SOUTHLAND
Auto Acres

A NOVEL
Lisa Jones

First published in the United States by Sticky Press in 2002 under the title *Up: A Novel*, ISBN 0971530904. Re-issued by Verbal Construction, LLC in May 2010 under the title *Southland Auto Acres*, ISBN 978-0-9826544-2-2.

This is a work of fiction. Names, characters, places, and incidents are either the product of the author's imagination or are used fictitiously, and any resemblance to actual persons, living or dead, business establishments, events, or locales is entirely coincidental.

Lisa Jones is a Denver native. *Southland Auto Acres* is her first novel. Under the pen name Beryl Barclay she wrote *Daily Scoldings: A Bracing Tonic of Criticism, Rebuke* and *Punitive Inspiration for Better Living*, published by Running Press in 2010.

Cover and interior design by Melissa Soukup.

verbalconstruction.com

chapter **ONE**

At the end of May I pointed my car west and went screaming over the Rockies, across the dry floor of an ancient Utah sea, through Las Vegas and the Mojave to stand here in a gray wool gabardine business suit and sell cars under the bright Los Angeles sun.

I came here because I wanted love. I wanted to own it. I succeeded, but not in the way I had hoped.

I succeeded in spite of myself. I stole a car. Actually, I thought I was stealing a car but I wasn't. I tried to kidnap Linnie, but she went along willingly. I had terrible sex with a guy at work. Joy threw me on her lawn and kicked me. All of this happened after I got the job selling cars at Southland Auto Acres in LA.

Maybe I should back up and explain a few things so my story will make sense. I should start with my sorority at the University of Colorado in Boulder—almost a year ago.

It was evening. My sisters and I were in the parlor of the sorority house for the final party of fall Rush. I was wearing pearls and a pink taffeta dress. I'd like to tell you that I looked good, like a debutante party girl circa 1957, someone glamorous and naughty. But I probably looked the way I felt—awkward, hesitant. Across the room, I saw one of my sisters put her hair behind her ear. This was our turnover signal, which meant, "Introduce yourself to this rushee so I can go talk to someone else." So I went.

"Meet Becky Pine."

That's me. I'm Becky Pine. The rushee's hand touched mine. My gaze wandered from her eyes down to her delicate mouth and slick teeth, down her slender neck, down her smooth, tanned breastbone to her nametag: Trisha.

It's one of those things that I kinda knew but didn't really acknowledge to myself: I find women attractive in a romantic way. That evening the fact slapped me like a clinical diagnosis. A thing can remain subterranean for a long time, but there comes a point when it's undeniable.

All the stories and rumors about lesbians that I had ever heard went streaming through my mind. For instance, Wallace and Kendra—oh, the drama! They were the infamous pair of Double Sig sorority sisters banished five years ago for an unspecified values violation, which means that they were caught having sex with each other in the shower. Their sorority pins had been officially lifted. Other than talking shit about you, lifting your pin is the worst thing a sorority can do to you.

Later that night when rushee Trisha's name came up in the scream circle, one of my sorority sisters declared: "Trisha Whitson has face. I want her."

"That girl was yum," said another sister. "You could eat her with a spoon."

Another sister screamed to signify her approval. More sisters screamed. The whole circle was literally screaming its lungs out for Trisha Whitson. Now tell me *that's* not mass hysterical lesbianism in hetero clothing.

Trisha ended up joining a sorority other than mine. I

spent the academic year thinking about how I could meet a woman with whom I could have an affair. I read a handful of "It's OK to be gay" books. I agonized about telling my parents. I drafted several "coming out" letters to my family but never sent them.

It wasn't until graduation day that I had a firm plan for becoming more than just a theoretical lesbian. On graduation night I drove down to Denver and went to a queer bar called Livid. My parents didn't protest when I told them that I couldn't join them for dinner. "There's a party I need to go to," I claimed, which wasn't exactly a lie.

So I went to Livid and met a woman named Marta from Los Angeles.

Marta from Los Angeles. Maybe it was the way she wore her makeup that made her look a little mysterious. I knew nothing about her so I was free to imagine her as perfectly seductive. One corner of her mouth was turned upward, almost imperceptibly, almost in a smirk. Her eyebrows were sharply tweezed, arched and dark. What I saw was an alluring, dangerous jungle cat.

We went to her hotel. Our footfalls clicked on the amber-colored onyx of the Brown Palace lobby floor. The sound drifted up six stories, past six tiers of cast iron Victorian balconies, past more than a hundred years of whispered history.

This is where they have the Denver Debutante Ball, I remembered. I pictured a succession of debs sweeping down the main staircase. Gowns rustling. A wave of white-gloved applause as each young woman was presented to proper society.

Marta and I walked up those stairs.

Her room smelled of cedar and dried rose petals, like a dresser drawer filled with lace. She stood in the dark, near the window, her head turned to one side. I gazed at her silhouette, the aristocratic slope of her nose, the curve of her lips. Was she just a shadow? I reached toward her, half expecting to touch nothing, half afraid my hand would splash through liquid darkness and scatter the illusion into ripples. I touched the backs of my fingers to her face. Her eyes glinted as she turned toward me. I felt the brush of her eyelashes on my cheek. Her sharp teeth. Her tongue like velvet, slick and warm. She knew what she was doing.

The next morning, I awoke to the sound of a knock.

Marta answered the door. Room service. A guy came into the room. He looked at me. He put the tray down. His eyes darted from Marta in her bra and panties to me, naked in bed. Marta scribbled on the check. The guy kept looking at me.

"That's right," I said. "We had sex. Go tell all your little busboy friends. We're here. We're queer. Get used to it."

The guy looked embarrassed.

Marta handed him the check. "Thanks."

He bolted.

"You're suddenly a lesbian activist?" Marta asked. "I think that's rude. It's rude to get in someone's face like that."

"It was rude for him to be staring."

"What do you expect? He's a guy. Guys get off on the whole thing." Marta poured herself a cup of coffee.

"That's a violation." I searched for my clothes. "I mean, doesn't that feel like a violation to you?"

"It's a compliment." Marta sipped her coffee. "Don't tell me you're a man hater."

"I don't know any men well enough to hate them." I picked up a coffee cup. Changing the subject. "I was thinking of maybe visiting LA this summer."

"You want cream?" Marta poured. "The women in LA are hot. There's a better selection than here. More options. Come to LA if you want. But don't get all hung up on me. I have a girlfriend. Didn't I tell you that?"

No, she hadn't told me. "No expectations." I put on my clothes. They reeked of stale cigarette smoke. They felt damp and sticky. "It would be nice if we could be friends." Not that I thought Marta would make a great friend. I just thought it would be nice to have lesbian friends in general.

"What's wrong with being good old-fashioned fuck buddies?" Marta smeared jam on a croissant. "Why do we have to be friends? Let's just be the sexual animals that we are and quit clouding the issue with all this shit about love and sisterhood and goddamn crunchy granola. Why do lesbians insist on turning each other into asexual teddy bears in Birkenstock sandals?"

I considered the question as Marta ate her pastry. Last night, Marta had seemed so much more beautiful. I began to suspect that I was capable of misjudging others and making unfortunate choices. "You have a point," I said. I drank the coffee. "I have to go. But I'll call you if I'm ever in LA."

"Yeah, please call. Just be discreet, OK?" Marta kissed my cheek.

I felt that she had dismissed me so I turned to leave.

"Hey." Marta grabbed my hand and pulled me back to her. "Everything dissolves just when you try to hold on to it," she said. She looked at me intently, in a way that reminded me of the night before. "Nothing lasts, Becky. We're in freefall. The best we can do is enjoy the ride." She sounded almost sad.

"Some things are worth holding on to, aren't they?" I asked.

She looked rueful. "Some things won't let go." She reached toward the room service tray. "Last night was fun. Keep this as a memento of our time together." She handed me a croissant. "It's a joke, Granola Girl."

"Thanks." I wondered when and how I had become Granola Girl. "Bye, Marta."

I walked down the hall to the elevators. I didn't want to take the stairs. I wanted to remember them the way they had been last night as Marta and I ascended. I wanted to preserve the memory of *anticipating* sleeping with her — it thrilled me more than the memory of actually sleeping with her. The croissant crackled in my hand.

The light above the elevator came on. The wood-paneled door slid open. The room service guy was standing in the car, alone. He smirked. "Going down?"

"Not with you." I turned to take the stairs.

"Lezzy."

I wheeled around. In one smooth motion, requiring no thought, no decision, I lobbed the croissant through the elevator door. It sailed in a wobbling arc and struck the guy's forehead. Buttery golden flakes shattered on impact. The door closed like the shutter of a camera, preserving forever his look of surprise.

Video cameras and an electronic security gate guard the driveway at my parents' house. The driveway curves through low hills covered with pine trees. Because of the pines, the house is hidden until you get to the circular drive. In the center of the circle is a heap of rocks straddled by a sculpture of a cowboy.

I parked under the guest carport. As I got out of my car, I touched the door to make sure the paint surface felt smooth. My dad would feel the smoothness to find out how often I waxed the car. Eddie Pine believes in preventive maintenance: If you take care of all the small things as you go, problems will never balloon to overwhelming proportions.

I didn't want to have to tell him, Dad, sometimes you can follow all the rules and do everything right and be the best parent ever, yet your kid comes home from college a man-hating lesbian activist. I have to be subtle and wait for the right moment, let the subject come up naturally, not force it.

I had heard stories about parents disowning their gay kids. I considered all of the standard movie-of-the-week plotlines: kid comes out, family freaks out then reconciles; kid comes out but it's no big deal; kid comes out and parents hire a cult deprogrammer to brainwash kid into heterosexuality. Anything is possible. Sometimes you don't know people as well as you think you do.

Slow and steady, I reminded myself as I dropped my book bag in the foyer. *No sudden moves, no rash statements.* I thought of all the "coming out" letters I had written and torn up. I wished I had sent one. I was sure that in at least one draft I had found the perfect words to say what I didn't want to say.

My mother had arranged a vase of fresh flowers in the hall. She could hire someone else to do it, but she enjoys doing cheery, homemaker-type things herself.

I remember once when I was a child someone asked me my dad's name. "Eddie Pine," I said. "What's your mom's name?" was the next question. I had to think about it. As far as I was concerned, Mom's name was Mom. She was so fundamental and constant like solid ground or fresh air that I didn't see her as an individual with an identity separate from her relationship with me. She was my mirror. When I hurt, she hurt. She studied me, dreamed about me and could talk to me without words. I was a miracle to her, even when I took her diamond wedding ring off her nightstand and dropped it down the furnace grate. That's when I realized that our relationship worked both ways—when she was upset, I was upset. As far as I was concerned, the worst thing I could do was make her cry.

She would probably cry if she knew why I was never interested in any of those nice boys she so diligently rounded up for me to date. How could I break it to her?

Yet how could I keep it from her? She's my mother, the

only person in the world who cares about me more than I do about myself.

"Mom, I'm home." I went into the kitchen.

I could hear her footfalls. "Ed," she said, her voice muffled, "Becky's home." There was probably a grunt of response that I didn't hear. Out of habit I opened the refrigerator.

My mom was wearing a purple golf outfit. She looked fabulous despite her attire, with a light tan, almost silver hair and a big smile. "There's leftover chicken casserole, or you could make yourself a sandwich," she said. "Look in the meat drawer. I think we have cheese. Or I could make some pasta for you."

I wasn't hungry. I let the refrigerator door swing closed. I turned and looked at her, at how happy she was to see me. I felt like an awful, dirty liar.

"How was your party, dear?"

I had also lied to her about my plans for the previous Marta-filled evening.

"I didn't go to a party, Mom. I went to a gay bar downtown and met a woman named Marta from Los Angeles and went back to her hotel and slept with her. I'm a lesbian. I always have been but didn't know it. There's nothing you can do about it. So I'm moving to Los Angeles tomorrow. That's just the way it is."

She gave a little yelp of surprise. I was surprised, too, that I had dropped the whole steaming mess on her all at once. Not to be crude, but she had wiped my butt when I was little — it seemed ridiculous for me to try to hide my shit from her now. I expected a torrent of tears. But she made a split-second shift from mother to parent. The look in her eyes went from one of extravagant, indulgent yet somewhat stunned love to one of equanimity. Her look told me that I had presented a serious matter requiring a serious and wise response. "I'm going to get your father," she said.

She left. I slumped into a chair. I heard her open the door to my dad's study, and I heard the door close. They were conferring. I should've told them both at the same time. I should've been more tactful.

Were they planning to punish me? I didn't know, didn't care. I just wanted out. I wanted to be in Los Angeles already, lounging on the beach under swaying palm trees. LA shimmered like an oasis in my empty future. LA was the answer to all my uncertainties. Sudden urgency pressed in my throat. I needed to get there as soon as possible.

My parents walked into the kitchen. They seemed fine. No tear streaks. No frazzled expressions. We sat around the kitchen table.

My dad was wearing the blue polo shirt that I had given him for Christmas. "Your mom tells me that you've had some things going on that I had no idea about," he said. "I'm glad that you know who you are. Not many people do."

"I don't know who I am exactly," I admitted. "I know more what I'm not. I'm not who I thought I was. I'm not who I'm supposed to be."

Mom jumped in: "Who is this young lady?"

"Mom, she's just some woman I met."

"I think we should meet this woman," Mom said, trying to be cool. "Since she is so important to you that you're uprooting your entire life and moving in with her."

"I'm not moving in with her," I said. "She already has a girlfriend."

Mom bristled. "She sounds exquisitely bad for you."

Dad was nervous. "So why are you moving to Los Angeles?"

I remembered what Marta had said about there being a better selection of women in LA. More options. "That's where the lesbians are."

"Are there no lesbians in Denver?"

"Oh, sure," I said, sarcastic, defensive. "Denver is crawling with lesbians, Dad. Just *crawling*." I wasn't able to explain that I felt confined by Denver. I wanted *more*. Something bigger. Somewhere new and challenging, a place to match the boldness I had begun to feel.

Dad took a new tack. "I guess my biggest concern is practicality. What do you plan to do out there?"

I hadn't thought about it. "I'll get into sales," I shrugged. "You always said that sales is a great thing to get into."

I felt my mom squirm.

I saw Dad restrain himself from shouting, *No. You can't. You have to stay here and do what I say.* He chose his words carefully. "Your mother and I have a lot of confidence in you. We know you can accomplish whatever you set your mind to. What do you plan to sell?"

I had no idea, of course, but when I thought of LA, the image that came to mind was a gridlocked freeway. "Cars," I said. "There are millions of cars in LA. Someone has to sell them."

He and Mom exchanged a look.

"Becky, you have a college degree," Mom said.

"I know," I said. "What difference does that make? I'm not saying that I'm going to sell cars for the rest of my life, but I have to start somewhere."

What I didn't say, though, was that the more I thought about it, the more intriguing the idea of selling cars was becoming to me.

"I have to be frank," Mom said. "This isn't the life we imagined for you."

"Mom, the life you imagined for me, and that I imagined for myself, was an *imaginary* life. I want a real life. My own real life."

After a long silence, Dad asked, "Does it have to be tomorrow, or can you wait until the day after?"

"I can wait a day, Dad, but I'm going. I'm definitely going." For the first time, I realized that what I was saying was true. I had made up my mind and my course of action was clear.

It's not as if there was nothing more to say. Maybe there was too much to say. But that's all we said that day about my news and my plans.

The oil in my car was clean. The paint was smooth as Marta's skin.

"That car's got a good little engine," Dad said. "You got your cell phone?"

"Yeah." In addition to a new phone, he had given me a lead pipe that I could barely lift, "for protection, just in case." He also handed me some cash and a check.

"Open an account first thing," he advised. "Establish a good relationship with your banker."

"OK, Dad."

"Call us if you need anything," Mom added. "Call us from the road. Call us later, OK?"

"OK." What great parents, I thought. Concerned about issues of practicality and the car-sales-in-California gambit much more than my sexual orientation. Perfectly wonderful parents.

I'm sure that they didn't take it as well as they had let me think. Of course they were upset. But there was nothing I could do about it. I had gone through my own anguish in throat-twisting silence, after all. It had been surreal to live in a sorority house full of group hugs, sisterly love, and delightful women aghast at the notion of lesbianism. If my parents were freaked out, I could understand. If they needed to cry, fine. But I had cried and kicked myself ever since I met Trisha Whitson. I was done with self-torture.

I began my trip in a euphoric stupor, insensible to the possibility of danger. I was on a mission.

I took a left turn out of my parents' driveway and headed for the Interstate. My route was marked on the map: West on Interstate 70; south on 15; then 10 west all the way to *The One*, Pacific Coast Highway. 70, 15, 10, 1 — a countdown to my new existence.

I drove alongside a river. Down the western slope of the

Rockies. Through Grand Junction. As I drove past the sign that said, "Now Leaving Colorful Colorado," my euphoria peaked. I looked in the rearview mirror. The terrain behind me was identical to the terrain ahead. Hot, dry, flat. I felt as if I had cleared mountainous hurdles only to see that I'd gotten, literally, *nowhere*.

I found a country music station on the radio. Songs about heartache and dust. A pickup truck roared past me. I watched it stretch away from me and vanish on the bleak horizon. Soon, billboards populated the emptiness: Last chance. No Services next hundred miles.

I stopped for a fill-up and a vanilla soft-serve—ice cream squirted into a beige cone. It had been my favorite summer treat when I was a kid. I stood in the sunshine and ate fast. Creamy drips merged into a sticky river down my wrist.

I felt pathetic, completely alone and anonymous, at a gas station in the middle of nowhere, trying unsuccessfully to revive a happy childhood memory, half wishing my mom would appear and swab me with a moist towelette. But I was on my own now, I reminded myself. *I'm living my life.*

Soon the music on the radio faded into a crackle of static. A dramatic landscape emerged: striped spires of rock; yawning, jagged canyons; wind-carved mesas. I was rolling across the parched, cracked floor of an ancient sea. The sun was sinking. The air looked golden, as if filtered through a glass of champagne.

Maybe it was the crushing heat, coupled with the fact that I'd been driving for eight hours. I became convinced that I was actually underwater, driving on the bottom of the ocean.

The depths pressed on the windows. The engine strained against invisible resistance. I tasted dampness and salt when I breathed. A huge prehistoric fish, fanged and armor-plated, swooped and snapped at the glittering lure of my car. I pulled over and hugged the wheel. My eyes squeezed shut. *If I open the door, I'll drown.*

After a few moments of mortal, hallucinatory terror, I raised my head. The wind kicked up a cloud of dirt in the distance. *Dry land.* I was safe. I got out of the car. The air hit my soaked shirt sending chills down my back. I walked a few yards.

I was near the halfway mark, halfway between Denver and LA I could turn around and go home. I didn't know what was ahead of me. Anything could happen.

I looked out at a silent ridge painted with layers of time. Eons and eons were stacked on top of one another like a slice of layer-cake eternity. The land looked like a billion years of waiting around, waiting for something—anything —to happen.

Why wait any longer?

When I looked back at the road it ran in only one direction as far as I could see. Forward.

I spent the night in a motel and arrived in Las Vegas the following morning. The Vegas strip had all the gritty heat and flash of a car lot. I was intrigued. I had never gambled.

In a crowded casino, an acid cloud of tobacco smoke whirled around me. Coins clanged into metal trays. The blinking name of a slot machine summoned me: Devil

Sevens. I sat down and fed a few bills into it. The number in the Winner Paid window registered my deposit. I felt as if I had already won something.

For the next hour I sat rapt in a meditative trance, pressing a button to spin the wheels and watching them stop. I won several small payouts. I expected to win an enormous jackpot. A jackpot would validate my choices and me. It would be a sign, an omen of good things to come. I would win on the next spin or the spin after that. *All it takes is one coin with the right vibration to trip a spring, click a lever and open the guts of this damn thing.*

As my stake dwindled, I re-examined my expectations. What difference would a jackpot make? My dad had given me a good sum to get started in LA. A jackpot would make me feel lucky. But in a very real sense I am already lucky. I've had the benefit of every advantage, every kindness a person could hope for in life. Even if my existence were utterly wretched, a jackpot might make my circumstances more comfortable but it could do nothing to, say, undo a cruel past or knit broken bones or bring a loved one back from the dead.

How foolish for me to abdicate responsibility for my happiness to a machine, I thought. *How stupid to look to a slot machine for validation. That's living in a fantasy world instead of the real world. Good fortune comes from within my own heart*, I told myself, *through my own actions.*

I had three credits left on my machine, enough for one last spin. Why not cash out? I had convinced myself of the futility of the game. Why spin one last time?

If I didn't take the spin, I would wonder for the rest of

my life: *What if this is my winning spin?* I wanted to have no regrets.

I mumbled an incantation that I had heard on campus: *Nam-myoho-renge-kyo.* It was alleged to be a lucky Buddhist mantra. *Nam-myoho-renge-kyo.* I said it again.

I pushed the button. The wheels turned.

I lost.

I nosed into breakneck traffic tearing west out of Vegas. Cars with California license plates whined past.

When I crossed the Nevada state line, a pack of motorcycles came out of nowhere and buzzed me like horseflies. They jockeyed and jumped from one lane to the other, rode my tail, cut around a big rig, then vaporized in the distance. Sparse clumps of gray scrub dotted the roadside. Soon the highway lanes multiplied. I merged onto the Santa Monica Freeway at rush hour, and was absorbed into a crush of cars snaking through what I imagined to be the colon of an urban behemoth.

Signs announced different cities, but there were no visible breaks or borders; each city spilled into the next. Every exit was choked. Emergency flares sputtered.

From a hill I saw downtown Los Angeles far away like a tiny castle floating on a cloud of smoke. Palm trees nodded. Flowers erupted. By the time I curved past downtown, the Hollywood Hills were shadowed blue. Traffic eased and accelerated. I shot out of a tunnel. The Pacific sunset splashed on my skin.

I had arrived.

I woke up twisted in sweaty sheets. Darkness hovered. I clasped my knees to my chest, searching the dull corners of my motel room. I heard the thrumming of the sea, the booming of the waves outside the door. I rocked back and forth, listening.

Sometimes I don't know when I'm dreaming and when I'm awake. If I had a girlfriend, I would know. I would look at her peaceful face and know that my nightmares are my own creation. I need a girlfriend to give me context. She would be a voice to echo mine, only more objective and with more wisdom. She would echo my best self, the part of me that's better than I think I am.

I heard the moan of a foghorn. I imagined a ship plowing blindly through emptiness. The sound reminded me of home, a thousand miles from any ocean. It was like a freight train pounding through Denver, the bluesy wail of its horn at 2 a.m., the song of being in the middle of nowhere, rolling somewhere, alone.

During my first full day in LA, I rented an apartment in West Hollywood, which, according to info that I had found on the Internet, was a gay-and-lesbian-friendly part of LA.

During my second day in LA, I was determined to land a car sales job. I drove down Santa Monica Boulevard past flashy dealerships. I was about to turn around and cruise the opposite side of the street when I saw Sweet Dream, a BMW convertible at Southland Auto Acres. I fixated on her.

I parked and walked up to take a closer look. I couldn't afford a new car and didn't need one. Still, I wanted her.

Gil, the smiling salesman in a suit, approached. "You don't want that heap," he said. "Take a look at the other side. It's hamburger."

Hearing him tell me that I didn't want the car only made me want her more. Gil was doing his job, trying to establish control over his Up. An Up is what car salesmen call a customer. In this case, I was the Up. A car salesman is often judged by how well he can lead his Up around the lot. So, understandably, Gil didn't want me to become attached to Sweet Dream.

I looked at the scratches and dents on the other side of the car. "I don't mind a few dings," I said. "It adds character. This car has a story."

"The story is that my manager is an ass," Gil said. "He won't send this beauty to the body shop. You're too hot to drive something that's, ah, not put together as well as you are."

"Whatever you're selling, I'm not buying."

His cocky smirk faded. "This is not an easy gig. Selling cars is hard work. But that's why I'm here. To work hard for you."

"I want to meet your ass of a manager," I said.

"You're going to complain about me? Let me make it up to you. Let me take you for a drive."

"I'm not going for a drive with you," I said. "I'm going to apply for a job. I can sell cars better than you."

Gil grinned. "You wanna bet money on that?"

"I'm not going to make a bet with you."

"Have you ever sold cars?"

"No," I conceded. "But I can sell *this* car to someone before you can," I said, pointing to Sweet Dream.

"You're on." Gil folded his arms and leaned on Sweet Dream. "If you sell this car, I'll buy you dinner. If I sell it, you'll buy."

"Either way, I'd be having dinner with you," I said. "That's no prize."

"The prize comes after dinner," he said. "But it's not going to happen. Squatty's not going to hire a ballwhacker like you."

"Someday, when I'm you're boss, you're going to regret this whole exchange." I marched toward the showroom. I had no idea what I was doing. I was determined to prove that jerk wrong.

Once inside the big glass doors, I walked past a row of offices known as the box. A nameplate on the last door read "Squatty." I could smell cigar smoke.

A large man cleared his throat. "What can I do ya for?" His eyes were runny.

"I'm Becky Pine. I'm looking for a job."

"When did you last see this job, ma'am?" He chuckled at himself. "Just tryin' to loosen you up. Sit down. Relax. Tell me about yourself."

I took a seat. What did I know about myself that I could

share with this wheezy man? What did I know about myself at all?

"I graduated from college."

He sighed. "I feel sorry for you higher-educated types. Your heads are all filled with crap. Every time you cram a new batch of facts into your head, you push out the God-given smarts that was already there." He lifted a pair of kitchen shears and snipped the end off a fresh cigar. "You got any practical skills?"

"In my sorority I learned how to meet and greet people."

He lit a match, held it to the end of his cigar and puffed. He didn't take his eyes off me. He didn't blink as he extinguished the match.

"What?" I asked, returning his stare. "I suppose you feel sorry for us sorority types because all our clapping and singing negatively impacts our ability to know shit from sugar puffs," I said.

In the silence that followed, I vaguely regretted my remark. My gaze wandered to the yellowish stains on Squatty's fingers.

He looked at his fingers and self-consciously rubbed the stains with his thumb. "Good," he said through his cigar-clenching teeth. "Real good. That's a crowd down. That's a skill ya can't teach."

Crowd down means two things. First, if an Up won't budge on a deal point, the salesman leaves the box and sends in a succession of salesmen or managers to rework the deal and wear down the Up's resistance. That's a basic crowd down. More liberally applied, crowd down means to stare at the Up and do nothing to fill an uncomfortable silence. The point is to force the Up into a submissive role. The person who speaks first loses the crowd down.

Squatty pushed himself away from his desk. "Let me show you the lot."

I followed him out the back door and through the car wash bay to the back lot.

He gestured to a car. "Know what that is?"

"A car," I said.

"Your college degree is payin' off already. What can ya tell me about that car?"

"I know nothing about it."

"Neither does your Up. So tell me something about it."

"It's red."

"It's claret," he corrected, pronouncing it "clarette." "Claret is better than red. You gotta build value. Enhance."

"It's claret. Which is associated with, um, the fine wines of the Bordeaux region." I winced.

Squatty was waving me on like a third-base coach. "More," he said. "Enhance. Enhance."

"A four-door large kind of sedan such as this one…is the one you should buy."

"No good," he said. "Never tell someone to buy something. Let them come to that conclusion on their own. You can lay 'em down but you can't make 'em sign the deal. You need some work, Becky Pine, but you got the basics." He launched toward the service garage. I followed.

"No demo, no draw, one day off a week," he said. "One weekend off per month and one bell-to-bell weekend whenever I say. You'll be able to pull in about a grand a week for yourself to start. Sometimes more. Sometimes less. Depends how hungry you are."

"Is that good?" I asked.

Squatty looked at me sidelong. "That's a good deal cuz I say it is. That's lesson one. I say what is and what isn't a good deal around here. More questions?"

By this time we were back in the showroom.

"Why do people call you Squatty?"

He rifled through a file cabinet, collecting a sheaf of paperwork for me to read and fill out.

"Name's Scott. My wife calls me Scotty. She's from Jersey so it sounds like she's saying Squatty—and damned if that ain't hilarity to your friends and casual acquaintances who hear it and pick it up and start calling you Squatty." He handed me the stack of papers. "The name stuck like shit on sugar puffs." He shot me a wink. "There are three crews of three. I'll put ya on Gil's crew. You'll learn how to sell a car from Gil. Selling a car is not something you can *think* about. It's something you gotta dig down and pull out of your gut."

He was referring to the lowest reaches of the intestine, I assumed.

"Selling a car is as real as this world ever gets."

I hadn't seen enough of the real world to contradict him. So I began my apprenticeship, as it were.

chapter **TWO**

I stood on the lot during my first couple of days thinking: *I sell cars. This is how I make my living.* I was appalled and impressed by this reality. I'm the only woman on the car lot, but Squatty calls me a salesman. "It's easier to think of you all," he says, "as salesmen rather than as persons."

Selling cars is mostly about standing around doing nothing. So I had plenty of time to think about the fact that I was utterly alone and girlfriendless. I felt a persistent longing. If I were to choose a car to serve as a metaphor for this longing, it would be a Volvo 240 DL, a boxy tank that will chug hundreds of thousands of miles and never die. That's what I drive. It's very safe, a roll cage on wheels. They don't make them anymore.

Because I had moved into a purportedly gay neighborhood, I had fantasized about a welcome-wagon greeting. I hoped that a motherly lesbian couple would knock on my door and give me Bundt cake. I imagined a sisterhood of women like woodland nymphs adorning me with flower garlands. There would be singing, dancing, as I was inducted into a lesbian society of mutual support. At the very least I expected a few friendly hellos. This was not to be.

West Hollywood was festooned with rainbow flags and Gay Pride stickers. Hordes of men congregated at bars and coffee houses along Santa Monica Boulevard.

But as far as I could tell, there were no lesbians. Where were the women?

I had purchased a futon that served as a bed and could be folded up to double as a sofa. I stretched out on my solitary piece of furniture and stared at the ceiling of my bachelor pad. I had one room in addition to a small bathroom, small closet and cramped kitchen. The plaster walls were webbed with earthquake cracks that a previous tenant had painted to look like grape vines. This added an element of bohemian charm.

I wanted to be a competent lesbian, so I needed to learn. When I wasn't at work, I was studying the sex manuals and queer-culture guides I bought at a gay bookstore down the street.

You'd think that because I am a woman, I would understand something about lesbian sexual Standard Operating Procedure. No. While I had a grasp of the biology involved, I knew little about time-honored techniques. Not only did this information fascinate me, it reminded me of my acute lack of lesbian friends and the dismally nonexistent state of my love life. Also, it suggested an answer to the question: Where are all the women? They're at home, presumably, doing *this*.

I didn't want to call Marta out of a sense of desperation. But I was desperate. I was worried that I would never meet any women. I would spend my days on the car lot and spend my evenings staring at the ceiling, the loneliest lesbian in Los Angeles.

I dialed her number. A woman answered.

"Marta?"

"No, it's Joy."

Joy—the committed, devoted girlfriend of the woman I had slept with.

"This is Becky Pine. Marta said something about getting together with you guys. I just moved here. She knows a lot of women in LA. I mean, she said I should call." *Why do I always feel compelled to explain and justify myself?* "I'm new. I'm a lesbian. I'm not sure what to do. I don't know anyone else."

There was silence. "Marta's not here," Joy said. "I'm sure she'd love to see you. We're meeting a friend for dinner tomorrow. Would you like to join us?"

I was stung by her gracious invitation. She was obviously a magnanimous person and I was a louse. "That would be great," I said. "Thank you." Joy gave me their address, and we hung up.

My gratitude swelled. But then a question arose: Why would Joy invite me, a total stranger, to her home without first consulting Marta?

I would go, but I would proceed with caution.

The next day, I stood among the rows of cars, looking at myself in the windshields, my reflection captioned: No Money Down, Low Mileage, Fully Loaded, Bargain Price. The new me.

I saw a station wagon whip a U-turn on the boulevard and pull up to the curb of the dealership.

"Incoming," I shouted, calling my first Up of the day.

I implemented the coaching that Squatty had given me. Smiling, I extended my hand. Squatty insists: "First thing, always shake hands with the customer. Once you touch 'em, you own 'em," he says.

"Welcome to Southland Auto Acres. I'm Becky Pine."

The Up took my hand limply and focused his gaze somewhere below my chin. He flicked his mustache with the tip of his tongue. "I'm just shopping."

As Squatty says, there's one thing to remember about customers: "No one comes to a car lot unless they want to buy, even if they say they don't. It's your job to make the moves and get the sale. It's the same as going to one of them singles bars. No one goes unless they're looking to get a little action."

At Southland Auto Acres, selling and screwing are interchangeable concepts.

"What can I show you?" I asked. "Cars? Trucks? Urban assault wagons?"

"My wife and I are thinking about getting a FamleeVan."

"You've come to the right place." Squatty Principle Three: *Always refer to a customer by his or her first name. Do it a lot.* "Your name is…?"

"Jim."

"Jim! We have over a dozen FamleeVans in the back lot, Jim. Just delivered yesterday, Jim."

Some salesmen use overly familiar permutations: Jimmy

Jimbo Jimster Jim-My-Man. And you're supposed to say something like, "Jim. That's a great name. My dad's name is Jim. Heck, my boyfriend's name is Jim, too. When I have a kid, I'm going to name him Jim. I even go to a gym."

We always tell our Ups that the car they want is in the back lot, a quarter-mile walk from the showroom. During the walk I'm supposed to qualify my Up — that is, find out if he can afford a new car, has he had any vehicles repoed, that sort of thing. Jim and I walked through a gantlet of glass and chrome. Sunlight seared off a bumper into my eyes.

Jim was an accountant from Manhattan Beach. I landed him on a fully loaded FamleeVan Grande XL. I said things like, "Jim, you're a successful professional, the kind of guy who'll settle for nothing less than the best...." Pumping him. He drove the FamleeVan around the block a couple of times and wanted to take it on the freeway.

All demos are risky, but freeway demos are the most dangerous. There's always a chance you'll get taken for a ride. That means your Up kills or rapes you or dumps you by the side of the road and steals the car. But if I refused to go on demos with potentially frightening customers, I wouldn't make many sales.

A perverse part of me wonders what it would be like if I took one of these cars on the freeway myself and just kept driving with no particular destination in mind. Maybe it would be like walking to the edge of a cliff, turning on my heel and dropping. No grasping for a lifeline, no dread of impact. Just freefalling. Just driving. This is my Job Escape Fantasy Number 12.

The demo was uneventful. This FamleeVan guy was looking like payday. When we got back to the lot I put him in the box. I gave him a cup of coffee from the vending machine. He sipped and stared at the DynoCoat Truck Bed Protection poster on the wall. It featured three women clad in plastic wrap: "Babes in Truckland," it read.

I went to the desk to run Jim's credit. Squatty smacked his mouth as if tasting something peculiar, puckering and unpuckering his lips like a mudsucking carp. He raised his eyebrows when he pulled the stock number.

"This is a biggie, Beck," he said. Think you can handle it? Squatty knew that price negotiation was my weakest suit. I was good at doing demos and getting customers to like me, but when it came down to price, I had no edge.

The strategy is to knock the Up off balance with a highball number and pretend that there's no room to move on the price. Then you do the go-between dance, acting as if you're negotiating with your sales manager on behalf of the Up. The whole point is to exhaust the Up into capitulation. Most car salesmen don't necessarily make more money for all the time and effort this strategy takes, but many of them do get a sadistic thrill out of it. Gil says he squeezes his Ups so hard they shit a nickel and shed a tear.

"I'll squeeze him, Squatty." I tried to convince myself as well as him. "This guy adores me. If he doesn't sign today, he'll be back. He has to talk to his wife."

"Be back is weaksuck greenpea talk," Squatty said. "I'll write the deal."

"But he's mine. I can do it. I need a whole deal."

"Half a deal is better than no deal. Get back on the line."

I hesitated. Squatty was right. I'd probably blow it. Half a deal is better than no deal. "But a whole deal would mean a bigger commission."

"Go," Squatty barked.

I slouched out of the showroom. I breathed the fetid heat. I had road grime on my teeth from smiling so hard. I waited for another Up. My hosiery felt sticky. I resented the Southland Auto Acres dress code. At almost every other lot, the salesmen get to wear khaki pants and polo shirts. But that's not "professional" enough for Squatty. I squinted as the sun carved deep lines into my face. We're not allowed to wear sunglasses either. Squatty says that sunglasses make us seem insincere. "Customers want sincerity," he says. "Even if you gotta fake it. Fake it 'til ya make it, that's what I say. Act like a good salesman and boom! You'll be a good salesman."

Yeah, right. You go to the Department of Motor Vehicles. You pay fifty bucks. They take mug shots, computerized laser fingerprints, DNA samples. You get your sales license and boom! You're the same asshole you ever were with a new credential for messing with people.

The once-ubiquitous sleazy salesman is becoming a fossilized oddity, however, thanks to online car merchants and no-haggle pricing at some dealerships. But there will always be tire kickers, people who show up on the lot with "no intention of buying." These are what Squatty calls The Flock, "sheep who need a shepherd." These are people who know they want something, but don't know what they want. My job as a salesman is to ferret out their desires and dreams. I paint a verbal picture of material and existential fulfillment behind the wheel of a car from our lot. Their eyes get all sparkly and their budgets get loose. According to Gil, it's a humanitarian service.

Car salesmen will do whatever it takes to get a deal. From intimidation to fabrication to begging, anything goes. Except skating. That's when you steal someone else's deal and refuse to split the commission money. If you skate, as Squatty says, "You might as well be a shark gushin' your own blood cuz all your buddies will eat you alive."

After a few minutes of watching the traffic roar past me, I turned around to face the showroom. Reynolds, the other salesman on Gil's crew, walked through the glass doors and stood at the end of the outdoor display platform.

"Heyya, Becky." Reynolds hopped down and walked toward me. Heat rose off the asphalt in watery, wavy sheets. The breeze from the boulevard traffic animated a few stray tufts of Reynolds' red hair, making it look as if his head was ablaze. The reddish-brown stubble on his chin made him look less boyish than usual.

"Gil sold another one, didja see that?" Reynolds said, disgusted. "Some rich laydown paid full pop. How can such a jerk close so many deals? Really chaps my ass, I can tell you that."

Reynolds ran his palms over his rumpled suit. It needed to be cleaned and pressed.

According to Squatty, Gil is the best salesman on the lot. He knows how to pack his deals and stroke his Ups. He has never made less than a grand on a sale, so they say. Naturally, Reynolds and I hate Gil's guts. He's blond, clean-cut, engulfed in cologne.

"Which one did he sell?" I asked.

"The brown Skyward with all the bells and whistles. Squatty'll spiff him double cash for unloading that ugly heap of crap. That car's been here longer than I have. Look at that. Breaks my goddamn heart," Reynolds said, wrinkling his freckled nose.

We watched as a comfortably retired couple shuffled out of the showroom to admire their new Skyward. Reynolds and I smiled and waved as they drove past us.

"Like taking candy from a senile millionaire," Gil said as he swaggered toward us. "I'm hot. What do you say, Beck?" He straightened his tie. His milky teeth glistened. His hair was bulletproof. "Wanna have dinner with a winner tonight?"

"No thanks, Gil."

"So what if you're a lesbian?" Gil said. "To celebrate diversity, I'll take you out and buy you a lap dance."

"For crissakes," Reynolds said. "She said no. Every day you ask her and every day she says no. Take a clue, Gil, wouldja, pal. This is getting embarrassing."

Reynolds sometimes assumed the role of my protective older brother. Flattering at first, annoying after a while.

Gil's eyes flashed with his brand of wicked glee. "The sale starts when the customer says no. If you were a decent salesman you'd know that, Reynolds."

"She doesn't buy the shit you're shoveling," Reynolds said.

"You can't make people do what they don't want to do."

"Reynolds, that's what salesmanship is. It's all about control. Selling means getting people to do what you want them to do. The only difference between rape and seduction is technique."

"You're so fucking ignorant," I said.

"You want it and you know it. I'm just trying to close the deal." Gil reached over and patted my ass.

This was an interesting moment for me. I almost lunged for Gil's eyes, prepared to avenge my gender, determined to punish him to the fullest extent of my fingernails. But I didn't. In Gil's mischievous smirk I saw the unmistakable flatness of someone who has no awareness of his own shitballness. Nothing I could do would change that.

I looked at myself from his point of view: To him, I was just some chick to harass, condescend to and try to fuck.

"Don't you worry about Gil, Beck." Reynolds gave Gil a sharp jab in the arm. "He's no threat. Got the smallest cock I ever saw. You could snip it off with a pair of manicure scissors. Show her, Gil."

I half laughed, disgusted by both of them.

Out on the lot, I heard a volley of shouts. Jim, my Up, stormed out of the showroom hounded by Squatty.

"No!" Jim said.

"Don't be a fool, Jimmy pal," Squatty persisted. "You'll never find a better deal."

"How many times do I have to say it? No!"

"C'mon, Jimbo buddyboo. What'll it take to sell you this car today? I can knock off another hundred but that's as low as I can go, rock bottom. I'll even throw in free floor mats," Squatty wheedled, scuttling alongside Jim like a barnacled crab.

Jim got in his station wagon and peeled away from the lot.

Unbelievable. Squatty had choked on the numbers. He is getting older, after all. I sighed.

But then I remembered how Squatty had dismissed me from the deal in the first place.

"There goes my rent, Squatty!" I shouted. "Thanks a lot!"

"If you'd done your job, we would've had a deal," Squatty snarled. "We had flat nothin'. And why? Cuz you're a weaksuck greenpea who doesn't know how to build value. You can't sell worth shit."

"That guy was ready to lay down, Squatty," Reynolds came to my defense.

"Squatty, the guy was an accountant or something," I said. "You can't pack the numbers and expect a guy like that to lay down. You blew him out of the box, not me."

"If it were up to you," Squatty said, "you'd give the damn things away." He lumbered back to the showroom, defeated.

"Man, that is really *transparent*," Gil said to me. "Reynolds is sticking up for you so he can get into your pants. At least I have the guts to come out and say what I really want." He looked over my shoulder. "Incoming Mustang. Mine."

He strode toward the curb.

Reynolds yelled: "Incoming family. Walking. Mine." He positioned himself on the display platform and greeted a young couple and their two kids.

In an instant I had lost a deal, two Ups, and some dignity. I clenched my fists, squeezing all my outrage into firm, manageable handfuls like icy snowballs. I muttered the mantra of transcendental frustration, "Fuck fuck fuck."

By the time I had walked to the farthest corner of the lot and gazed a while at the lulling traffic, my anger had subsided. The sun glared down and I glared back. I stood next to Sweet Dream, the convertible BMW at the front of the Southland Auto Acres used car section.

From one side, Sweet Dream looks like golden cream puff, fully loaded. But on the other side she's battle-scarred with sideswipe streaks, dents and a long gash. Squatty insists that someone will buy her as-is, so he won't invest in repairs. It's an experiment to prove elements of his elaborate car-based philosophy of life, which he expounds daily and unsolicited.

Squatty says that the reason people buy used cars is so they can satisfy their deep need to rescue and redeem that which has been cast aside. He thinks that someone will buy Sweet Dream for the same reason that people rescue dogs from the pound or buy puppies that are, by puppy standards, disadvantaged. People love to be rescuers.

Scars and all, there's something about Sweet Dream that makes my eyes gleam and my heart swell. The first time I saw her I wanted to buy her on the spot. I had no good reason for wanting her but I wanted her just the same. So maybe Squatty's right about not sending her to the body shop.

I leaned on Sweet Dream and watched Reynolds for a while. He was developing a rapport with his Up, addressing some of his patter to the little kids who were pretending to drive one of the cars. I hoped he would write a deal on this Up.

Reynolds sleeps in one of the custom vans in the back lot. He keeps all his clothes in the back seat of his car. His fiancée threw him out of their condo, Reynolds confided to me once, but he didn't say why. I think that if he would floss his teeth more regularly it would make a world of difference to the people in his life.

Reynolds was nice to me right from the start. During my first week, other salesmen would say, "Hey, greenpea. Check out a few stock numbers for me, willya?" Or, "Greenpea, go find out about the new trucks." I was happy to oblige, rushing all over the lot. I thought I was being helpful until Reynolds pulled me aside and said, "Kid, don't let them throw you under the bus like that." Using a ruse to keep other salespeople off the line, thus reducing competition for Ups, is known as throwing them under the bus.

After an hour or so, Reynolds was still doing well with his Up. He'd demoed two FamleeVans so far. He could make a good paycheck on the deal. Other than that action, the lot was dead. Gil's Up had walked before he'd even demoed a car.

I stood in the shade near the display platform and yawned. Squatty must've seen this. He came toward me.

"You wanna be a good salesman, Beck? You gotta watch Gil. He's hungry. He's got a big ol' tapeworm in his belly."

"I'm sure he has," I said.

"You don't like Gil, do you? A little sexual tension's all that is."

"I'm a lesbian, Squatty. You're creating a hostile work environment."

Squatty gnawed his unlit cigar. He gazed out at the boulevard. "Why do you have to give things names?" Flecks of tobacco stuck in the foamy corners of his mouth. "Nice young girl like you. Why can't you just be who you are without calling it something?"

"I'm a nice young girl. That's the label you like. *Dyke* is a good label too. More accurate. Why don't you use that?"

Gil walked toward us. "You got a phone call, Squatty."

"Hostile work environment," Squatty clapped Gil on the back as he headed for the showroom. "That's a ten-dollar way of saying car lot."

Gil smirked. "Someone's going to have an unpleasant surprise. You'll see," he said. "Bad news for Reynolds."

"Not quite. Reynolds has a strong Up."

"Yeah, too bad." Gil whistled tunelessly for a few moments. "Toooo bad."

"What's too bad?" I hated to give him the satisfaction of my curiosity but I wanted to know.

"Reynolds is going to put his Up in the box, write a gravy

deal, and not make a dime for himself. That jerkoff let his sales license expire. You can't sell a car without a license. If he writes a deal, it'll be a house deal. His name won't be on it. He won't make a dime."

"Why didn't Squatty tell him?"

"Squatty'd be pissed if he found out. Reynolds is a big boy. He oughta know when his license needs to be renewed."

"So how do you know this?"

"Beck, I make it my business to know everything there is to know about this car lot." He declared this with such pride and confidence that I believed him.

I walked to the back lot and Gil followed. I caught Reynolds' attention and explained the situation in an urgent whisper.

"No way," Reynolds hissed. "I renewed it last year."

"You have to renew it every year, jerkoff," Gil said. "Don't worry. I'm willing to close your deal for you while you go to the DMV."

"Forget it, Gil. I need a whole deal. Besides, I don't trust you."

"C'mon, Reynolds. Half a deal is better than no deal. I can get gravy. I want this deal as much as you do," Gil said.

Of course I was suspicious. But Gil was hungry; he might get twice as much as Reynolds could. That way, half a deal would be just as good as a whole one.

That's probably what Reynolds was thinking as he glanced over at his Up. The entire family was beaming, sitting in the van as if they already owned it. "OK," Reynolds conceded.

"But no skate."

Gil raised his open palms. "No skate."

Reynolds was gone long enough for Gil to push the deal through the desk and out the door.

Reynolds returned in time to wave as the family pulled away from the dealership in their new van.

"He threw me under the bus!" Reynolds said. "I didn't need to renew it."

"Did he skate you?" I asked.

"Nah, he'll have to split the money. Just makes me look stupid."

"Congratulations, Reynolds," Squatty said as Reynolds and I stepped through the big glass doors of the showroom. "You got half a deal."

"Damn funny, Gil. Got half my deal. Slithering asswipe."

"It was fun, pal, but it wasn't worth it," Gil said. "Don't spend your twenty-five bucks all in one place."

Gil had lowballed the customer and had written a pathetic deal just to screw Reynolds.

Squatty chided Reynolds: "Don't go disappearing in the middle of a deal. And *you*," Squatty pegged Gil. "You are losing your bite."

Gil shrugged. "I'll make up the difference on my next deal." He watched for something other than shock to register on Reynolds' face.

"Twenty-five dollars?" Reynolds said. "Twenty-five crummy bucks?"

"Becky, babe." Gil winked. "Thanks for all your help."

Reynolds' eyes widened, hurt and sad, as if I'd stabbed him in the heart. Dazed, he walked outside and sat on the edge of the display platform, his head in his hands.

I debated whether to go sit next to him. I pitied him, of course, but I also felt pain of my own. I despaired at the frailty of my good intentions compared to the cruel machinery of car lot reality. And yet I chose to work here. I wanted to be here. I had swooped into this place like a swan onto a lotus lake. What the hell was I doing?

As I looked at Reynolds, I saw my own face reflected in the showroom glass. How can I learn to care about other people without getting sucked into their bullshit? How can I learn to care about myself without becoming a narcissist?

If I were a freight train I'd blow my lonely whistle at this particular juncture. *Get off the tracks! I'm plowing through without a fucking clue.*

Marta and Joy lived in a Craftsman bungalow off Santa Monica Boulevard several blocks from my apartment. Their lawn, shaded by a magnolia tree, sloped up to a well-tended flowerbed. Rosebushes bloomed in front of the windows. On my way, I had stopped to buy a bottle of wine. I was glad I had chosen the more expensive merlot. I wanted to make a good impression.

I rang the bell. A dog yapped inside the house. I pictured a tiny poodle like a puff of cotton candy wearing a rhinestone collar.

"Yes, Cyril." I heard light footsteps on a hardwood floor. "Who's that, Cyril? Who's that?"

"It's Becky Pine."

The door opened. A petite woman with short brown hair looked at me through geek-chic glasses. Her eyes were hazel and intense. "Yes, I assumed it was you," she said. The dog, which was a poodle, danced in circles at her feet.

Joy did not invite me in. She just looked at me with a calm concentration that unnerved me. I would later learn that she was a successful attorney known for her gentility and dispassionate ruthlessness.

"I brought wine." I held up the bottle.

She gestured for me to enter.

I stepped inside.

She took the bottle from me and glanced at the label. "Ah, this one. Marta is getting ready. Would you like something to drink?"

"Some wine?" I shrugged.

"Make yourself at home." She slid the bottle I had given her into a wine rack against the wall. She walked into the kitchen. "Linnie is on her way."

Marta and Joy's living room was filled with antique Stickley furniture. It looked like a museum of the Arts and Crafts movement. Ella Fitzgerald singing Gershwin wafted through the house. Cyril, the poodle, ran from the kitchen to the living room and back again, his paws clicking on the hardwood floor.

An embroidery hoop rested on the coffee table. It looked as if Joy had just been doing needlework. I noticed several needlepoint pillows with different designs involving dragonflies. Afghans were draped over the backs of chairs. I assumed that Joy had knitted them. A strange, *Little House on the Prairie* hobby for a young, hip lesbian professional, I thought.

Joy returned and handed me a glass of white wine. "I think you'll like this chardonnay," she said.

I took it from her. "Thanks." Wondering, not daring to ask, *What was wrong with the wine I brought?* I could feel my face flush. Had I committed a *faux pas*? I perched nervously on the arm of a chair.

"Please have a seat," Joy said. She indicated a chair across the room from where I was perched.

As I moved to comply with her request, I realized that she was pulling a Gil. I was an Up. Joy was asserting dominance over her turf.

"Did you do all this needlework?" I asked. "It's fabulous."

"Thanks. I find it relaxing." She sipped her wine and looked at me. "So. How did you and Marta meet?"

Marta's warning for me to be discreet rang in my ears. "In Denver," I said. "In passing." I took a drink. "Yes, this is quite good. Good choice."

"Linnie is a dear friend of ours," Joy said.

I was relieved that she didn't pursue the topic of Marta.

"One thing that I want to advise you about — so you don't get the wrong idea. It can be easy to get the wrong idea. Linnie is straight. She's heterosexual. Fully and totally. I mention this so you won't be under the impression that we're setting you up in a love situation."

"Oh, no, I mean, I have no expectation like that," I said, which was a lie. Of course I was hoping that Marta and Joy would introduce me to a world of eligible bachelorettes.

"Linnie is lesbian friendly," Joy explained. "She likes to go to gay bars. She likes to flirt. She doesn't mean anything by it. I've seen women go off the deep end for her. But she's not interested in women. She lives with a man."

"I get the message," I said.

"I just want you to know," Joy continued. "If she flirts with you, it doesn't mean the same thing to her as it means to a lesbian. Don't read anything into it."

"OK," I said. I didn't like that Joy was trying to control my perception of Linnie before I had even met her. "Thanks for the heads up."

The sound of the doorbell threw Cyril into a frantic dance. Marta emerged from a hallway. "Becky, you look great." She reached for the door.

As Marta whooshed past, I didn't get a good look at her. Her presence did nothing to raise my pulse, though. She seemed to regard me the same way. Whatever spark there had been between Marta and me in Denver had completely burned out. I was glad about this, too, because otherwise I would have feared Joy's relentless, vengeful politeness all night.

"Linnie, sweetheart!" Marta said.

Slim. Blonde. Linnie. She kissed Marta full on the mouth. "I missed you!" Then she turned to Joy, who rose to meet Linnie's kiss. "Joy, my darling, darling."

"I'm Becky." I stood and extended my hand preemptively. I did *not* want Linnie to plant a kiss on me.

I did *not* like her. I did not like her showy, affected smooching. I did not like her tight jeans and tight T-shirt. I did not like her fresh, Scandinavian-model face or her hair in a ponytail, or her neck, all smooth and long, like a ballet dancer. I didn't like how obviously, naturally beautiful she was. Undoubtedly she was a horrible person. No one could appear so pure and not have a heart full of rotting sewage. I needed to dislike her to ward off her diabolical power. She was perfect for me.

She shook my hand. It was the briefest of handshakes. As a car salesman, I had shaken hands with all kinds of people. This handshake was different. There was *something* there. I don't know if Linnie looked the same way I had looked when I shook Trisha Whitson's hand at the sorority rush party. Maybe she did.

"Sorry," I said. I was sorry for the palpable awkwardness between us.

Linnie pulled her hand away from mine. "Nice to meet you."

Marta and Joy traded a look.

"How is Samuel, Lin?" Joy asked. She seemed to put a lot of emphasis on the name Samuel.

"Great," Linnie said. "Still in New York."

"Let me get you a glass of wine." Joy, followed by Cyril, went into the kitchen.

"Samuel and Joy work together," Linnie explained to me. "They're lawyers. That's how I met these guys. Through Samuel. My boyfriend."

"Your boyfriend," I repeated, to let her know that I acknowledged this badge of her devout heterosexuality.

"We would've run into each other eventually," Marta said. "Lin and Samuel's house is just two streets over. Plus, she likes to go out to the bars." As she explained this to me, Marta put her arm around my waist. "Becky is a newbie, Lin. We have to show her around town." She gave me a squeeze.

Joy returned from the kitchen with Linnie's wine. Marta edged away from me. I thought I saw a flicker of resentment in Joy's eyes. But it was hard to see her eyes, let alone detect emotional nuances in them. Glare on her thick glasses kept me guessing. At times I felt that Joy was glowering at me. Maybe this was due to my guilty conscience rather than any real glowering.

"Where are you from?" Linnie asked me after a while.

"Denver," Marta answered for me and insisted that we walk a few blocks to the restaurant.

As the four of us walked, Joy made sure to stay alongside me. Joy's manner reminded me of that saying, "Keep your friends close and your enemies closer." We walked behind Marta and Linnie.

Joy and I discussed lawn care. I told myself that Linnie wasn't my type. I wasn't attracted to her. She was too womanly. I compared her with Marta, who was also *womanly*, but not as much as Linnie.

"Your roses are beautiful," I told Joy. "Do you prune them yourself?"

What the hell did I mean *by womanly*? Any definition would be subjective, dictated by my tastes and expectations. *Womanly is what I find attractive in a woman. A woman I consider to be womanly is somehow my ideal of womanhood, my dream woman. Not that Linnie is my dream woman. I mean, not necessarily.*

"We have a gardener," Joy said.

Marta seems less womanly compared to Linnie because I am less attracted to her. Why had I slept with Marta? It was because of the circumstances at the time rather than any overwhelming attraction. What if she's looking at me and thinking, Why did I sleep with Becky? How terrible. It's impossible to know what other people think unless they come right out and say it. Even then, people are good at deception. I mean, I think I know what motivates me, but maybe I'm deceiving myself. I can only observe and assume. Why not assume the best?

I was checking out Linnie the whole time but I guess Joy thought I was checking out Marta. Joy had a firm frown on her face. Her lips were tight, seemingly bottling up a fierce tirade. Maybe that was why I perceived Joy as controlling. Her every muscle seemed tense, as if she were holding a wild elephant on a leash and trying to make it heel.

"I like having a beautiful garden," Joy said. "But I don't

have a knack for it. As long as it looks good, I'm happy. I don't want to get my hands dirty."

She was certain, I assumed, that Marta and I had had an affair in Denver. Joy was probably wondering if the affair had ended. And if it had ended, why had I come to LA?

Apparently, Joy and Marta had an understanding. To keep Marta in her life, Joy would have to allow Marta to do whatever she wished with whomever she wished, I assumed. Their relationship was a partnership between independent, mature adults, not some soppy codependent romantic fantasy. Yes, there was love—adult love, respectful love, with no unseemly jealousy or pining.

"I've noticed that as people get older, they like to garden," I said. "I think that's because older people have learned to be more patient. Gardening takes patience and nurturing."

"It's not very sexy, is it?" Joy said. "Gardening."

Joy was pining all the time, probably, changing her schedule to accommodate Marta's whims. She was in love with Marta, I guessed—and Marta told herself that she loved Joy too, especially, say, when Joy flew them to Paris on the spur of the moment. The only difficulty in their relationship, in Joy's eyes, was the blight of opportunistic young women like me who threw themselves at Marta.

"No, I wouldn't call gardening sexy," I said.

"No," Joy repeated. "Not sexy. Not at all."

Joy probably thinks I'm nothing more than a stupid, inexperienced, unpolished girl. Pretty and brainless. Mercifully brainless. If I had a brain or any decency, I would not have come to Joy's home. I would not have invaded Marta's life.

It was too sad. Their relationship wasn't about love and trust, it was about practicality and contractual obligation. I could see how Marta and Joy would both resent that on some level. Why bother staying together? One thing that Marta had said echoed in my mind, "Some things won't let go."

Marta and Linnie were walking several feet ahead of us but I overheard bits of what they were saying. I was doing some creative listening.

"So what do you think?" Marta asked. "She's hot, right?"

"Why do you ask me every time? On what am I supposed to base my evaluation?" Linnie lowered her voice. "Are you having an affair with her?"

"She's not my type. Zero attraction."

I wanted to protest. But then Marta said: "Maybe she's *your* type."

I didn't hear the answer.

Marta laughed. "If you haven't fallen for me by now, you're lesbian-proof." She turned around and asked Joy, "Isn't Linnie the straightest woman you know?"

Joy said, "I don't know. I was just thinking that maybe Linnie and Becky deserve each other."

At the sushi restaurant, Marta picked a table in the corner under a pink neon sign that read, "Eat it raw." Marta and Linnie sat next to each other. Joy sat next to me. I was able to look right at Linnie, but I looked at everything except her. We ordered food, sake and beer.

We talked for a half hour about movies. I was surprised at

how knowledgeable Linnie was. Because she was so pretty, I was almost hoping that she would be stupid — that would provide some sort of cosmic balance, I thought. I tried to interject smart-sounding comments into the conversation. I think I came across as nervous and self-conscious — which was how I felt.

Face to face, Linnie seemed to scrutinize me. "Do I make you uneasy?" Lin asked.

"Not at all," I said, defensive yet impressed at her forthright approach. "I mean, kind of. Sorry. Yes. Does that make any sense?"

"No," Joy said.

"It's like we have a connection," I explained, feeling exposed. "Like I recognize you or something."

Linnie nodded.

"Linnie's used to that," Joy said. "Everyone thinks they have some deep connection with her. It's so pathetic. Lesbians don't know the difference between infatuation and love."

I hated Joy's smugness. "What *is* the difference?" I asked.

"Infatuation is all about craving and grasping and needing to cling to her," Joy said. "Love is when you can hold a woman in your heart and not need to hold her in your hand."

I didn't roll my eyes, but I wanted to.

"Linnie has the Straight Woman Mystique," Marta explained. "Every lesbian fantasizes about converting a straight woman."

"Every lesbian except the ones who have done it," Joy added. "Believe me, it's gratifying at first but the novelty wears off fast. Plus, inevitably, your affair will end in tragedy." She seemed to be explaining this specifically to me. "No one ever stays with her first lesbian lover. When she dumps you it's like a hammer through your skull, Becky. Wrecks your head forever." I assumed she was speaking from experience.

"You never want to be a woman's first lover," Marta said. "She'll be clueless and need tons of supportive bullshit from you. Then, just when you fall in love with her, she'll dispose of you like old tuna salad. All of a sudden she realizes that she's looking at a gourmet buffet of sexual opportunity. She wants to eat a little bit of everyone."

I'm not sure if it was one specific thing that was said or if it was more of an aggregate — the words, inflections, facial expressions and body language — whatever it was, I became aware that the four of us were enveloped in a caustic cloud of cynicism that made my eyes water. Marta and Joy knew all there was to know about life and lesbians. How much of their posturing was self-protective, I'm not sure. But they were beyond jaded and well into jaundiced.

I wondered if I had told Marta that she was the first and only woman I had ever been with. I didn't think so. I hoped not. Still, I wondered if her remarks were pointed at me. Was she trying to tell me something?

"If I were a woman's first lover, I would feel lucky," I said. I stared at my beer. I could feel everyone's attention on me. "No one knows how long a relationship is supposed to last or what it's supposed to look like. If someone opened herself to me that way, I would want to be open to her too. I would want to be completely naked, emotionally defenseless."

Joy smiled, pitying. "I too was once naïve," she said. I felt her hand on my knee. At first, I thought she was making a pass at me, but then she squeezed. Her fingers were strong, bruising, digging into the bone.

"Shit, Joy. That hurts."

"Damn straight it hurts." Joy let go. "You'll get the stuffing kicked out of you and you'll wise up. Here. Try this." Between her thumb and index finger, Joy held a cup of sake. "Banzai!" She dropped it, cup and all, into my full glass of beer.

I recoiled.

"It's a sake drop. Try it."

I took a sip. It was awful.

"A Japanese boilermaker. Good, huh?"

I noticed that she didn't put any sake in *her* beer.

Linnie offered me a look of sympathy.

"Becky, tell us about your job," Joy said. "What do you do?"

"I sell cars."

No one responded. No shock, no curiosity. Just *nothing*.

"New and used," I continued. "At Southland Auto Acres. It's my first real job, so I'm, like, starting in the mailroom of life."

"A mailroom would be a step up," Joy said. "Is it

unbearably sleazy? Or do you fit right in?"

"Both," I said. "It's sleazy and I fit right in."

"I don't believe that," Linnie said. "There's nothing sleazy about you, Becky. You're straightforward as a gunshot and just as scary."

I almost thanked her, but I couldn't speak because I was suddenly embarrassed and choked.

"Becky is *scary*?" It was the most hilarious thing that Joy had ever heard. "Absurd!"

"I mean there's something genuine about you, Becky," Lin said. "Everyone has their shtick, you know, the story they want to tell you about who they are. As if they're afraid to let you figure it out for yourself. It's impressive when you meet someone who isn't interested in controlling the spin." She looked at Joy. "Besides, Samuel says that sales skills are the key to success in any field. Even lawyering."

Samuel again. "My dad says the same thing about sales," I offered.

"See, Lin, I always said that Samuel is like a father figure," Marta needled.

"Samuel is my boyfriend," Linnie explained to me. Again.

"Does he like to go out to lesbian bars with you?" I asked.

"He's a dud," Marta shot. "A *loaded* dud."

"He's a gifted attorney," Joy said. "And a dazzling intellect."

"He doesn't like to go out," Lin confessed. "But he likes for me to have a good time."

Hmm. How *generous* of him, I thought.

"I'd love to take you out," Linnie said to me. "I find it liberating to dance with women."

I figured it was one of those "let's do lunch" things. But she pushed it.

"Here," she handed me the sushi menu/checklist and a pencil that the waitress had left on our table. "Give me your number. I'll call you."

Joy raised an eyebrow at this.

I was focused on Linnie's cool blue eyes, and the way she was trying to look provocative, maybe, as if *daring* me to give my number.

I wrote it down. "This is going to be my first LA social lesson, right? I give you my number and I never hear from you again."

"I'll call you," Linnie said. "I will." She took the piece of paper, folded it and stuffed it in her pocket. "You have trust issues," she said with mock seriousness.

"We all have trust issues," Joy said. "Trust is something you have to build with another person over time and through difficult circumstances. You can't expect the other person to behave in a trustworthy manner just because you have a reasonable expectation that they will. You can't tell others how to behave. *You* have to be the change you wish to see in your relationship."

"Thanks, honey," Marta said. "That's profound."

For a minute I thought Marta was being sarcastic, but then she and Joy clasped hands over the table.

I'm willing to grant that there was a level of complexity

or depth to Joy and Marta's relationship that I could not possibly understand, let alone judge. And maybe I do have trust issues, because I was very suspicious of them. To me they seemed more like car salesmen than lovers. I wondered if the women who happened to fall into their orbit — such as Linnie and I — were Ups, objects for them to scorn and manipulate.

At the end of the meal, Joy made a great show of not making a great show about picking up the check and treating us all to dinner.

As I walked home, I thought about Linnie — about her beautiful, kissable mouth. I thought about her slender fingers folding the paper with my phone number on it, and how this paper was now in her hip pocket, warm with her body heat.

I hoped that she would call but I assured myself that she wouldn't. *Linnie is straight,* I reminded myself. *Well, maybe not straight. Just unavailable. But is anyone ever available? Look at Marta. She seems available to everyone but Joy. Maybe "available" is another way of saying, "conveniently, mutually attracted with no obstacles." Yet when does that ever really happen?*

I followed this line of thought because it kept me from obsessing specifically about Linnie and the fact that she would never, ever, ever call me. Never. In fact, I didn't *want* her to call. Damn Linnie with her damn Samuel. I would hang up the phone if she ever dared call.

chapter THREE

On Friday morning, Squatty and I stood around watching a group of men raise a red-and-white striped tent above the car lot.

"You ain't selling enough cars," he said. "You're trying too hard. In a tent sale, you won't have time to try. The lot's gonna swarm with Ups." He took his cigar out of his mouth and wiped his bluish nose on his shirtsleeve.

"What do you mean trying too hard?" I squinted back at him.

"You're too concerned about what the customers want and what they think about you. That stuff don't mean crap."

This seemed contrary to the gospel of the Southland Auto Acres sales manual, *Sell Cars and Everybody Wins*.

"What about serving customer needs? What about selling myself?" I asked.

Squatty laughed, a sound half way between a cough and a shout. "Gil sells more cars than anyone. Do you think he cares about that crap?" He flashed his ochre teeth. "Gil cares about Gil. That's what sells cars." He hooked his thumb into his waistband and rocked on his heels. "You gotta detach yourself. You gotta quit grasping. Concentrate on the flow of the out breath."

He paused to let his Squatty-dharma sink into the depths of my being. I attributed his philosophical nature to the fact that he had spent decades on car lots staring at traffic. This must be a form of meditative discipline.

"Lookie there!" Squatty stabbed his cigar in the direction of a man who was wheeling a hot dog cart onto the lot. "We got a weenie machine."

There was a popcorn cart, too, and strings of bright plastic pennants that looked like Tibetan prayer flags. Helium balloons like bunches of huge latex-skinned grapes hovered over the lot. A banner flapped in the boulevard traffic breeze, "Carnival of Cars."

Carnivals enchanted me when I was a child. An ordinary neighborhood park would be transformed for a night into whirling colors, lights, sticky sweets, games and rides—a magical dream. Then you grow up. You notice the licentiousness of the man who runs the Ferris wheel. You catch a tangy whiff of booze and urine as you walk past a tent. You realize that carnivals are seedy and sad. Naturally, car dealers have embraced the motif.

"Car Warehouse over on La Brea has an enormous inflatable gorilla on its roof," I said. "Weenies can't compete with that."

"It's not just weenies, Becky," Squatty explained. "It's cheese dogs too."

I pictured the aforementioned meat product, engineered with a hollow center and injected with liquid cheese food. "Cheese weenies," I said. I liked the way it sounded.

The public address speakers crackled, "Sales. Line one."

"Take the Up," Squatty said.

"No thanks," I said. "I never get there fast enough." When a phone pop was announced, salespeople would rush the showroom, climbing over one another to reach the telephone, like seagulls fighting over a potato chip.

"It's a potential customer," Squatty barked. "Take the Up."

I went into the showroom and was surprised to see line one still flashing.

"Hi. Thanks for calling Southland Auto Acres. This is Becky Pine, your personal sales consultant. What can I do for you?"

"I'm looking for a Violator QZ," a guy said. "I saw them at the car show. You have any?"

"Sorry. Not until next month. Want me to call you?"

"Yeah, sure."

I logged the guy's name and number onto the phone-pop sheet. I frowned as I walked toward Squatty. "He wanted a Violator," I said.

"When's he coming in?"

"He's not. I told him we don't have any yet."

Squatty groaned. "You can't sell a car if you got no customer on the lot. To hell with what he wants to buy. Sell him what you want to sell him. That's what selling *is*."

"But, Squatty, that would be lying."

Squatty paced back and forth in front of me. "You told that guy we weren't interested in selling. You told him to buy somewhere else." He stopped pacing and squinted toward the curb. "See that incoming walker?" He pointed at a man in a business suit. "Take the Up. Tell him we won't sell him a car."

"Squatty, don't be ridiculous. It's not the same."

"Sure as hell is."

In the distance I could see Gil moving toward the Up.

"This one belongs to Becky," Squatty yelled. "Get back on the line."

Gil backed off.

"Don't sell him a car, Becky," Squatty threatened. "Don't you dare." He planted his cigar in his mouth and folded his arms. This was to be another one of his Up-psychology exercises.

Last week he told me to climb into the trunk of every car I demoed. "Customers want you to be wacky," he had said. "Climb in. Sit down. Invite the Up to join you." The technique sold maybe one car and destroyed three pairs of my hosiery.

I hurried to intercept the Up at the curb. "Hi," I said, extending my hand. "I'm Becky. I'm afraid I can't sell you a car today."

The guy didn't shake my hand. Above his sunglasses, his heavy eyebrows creased. "I'm just looking." A smile stretched across his face and stopped before revealing his teeth. Maybe it was a sneer.

"I *can* help you look." Squatty hadn't prohibited that. "You strike me as a fun-loving guy, Mister, uh…" He started walking toward the back lot. I lengthened my stride to catch up with him. "Maybe a convertible, Mister…."

"Doctor."

He was tall and gangling with a shaft-up-his-ass walk, like a marionette on a stick. I could hear his breath hiss through the thick hairs sprouting from his nostrils.

"Doctor of what?" I asked.

His voice was low and even. "Doctor of none of your goddamned business."

Gil was following several yards behind us so I signaled for a turnover.

It happens. People come onto the lot with their defenses up, thinking that if they're not rude bastards, the salespeople will lay 'em out. As if assholishness would ever hurt a car salesman's feelings.

Gil swooped in. I was glad to see the predatory glint in his eye.

I walked toward the boulevard. Reynolds was standing on the line. He'd been sulking ever since Gil threw him under the bus with the DMV sales license ruse. I had tried to explain that I wasn't in cahoots with Gil. But Reynolds would just shrug. I think he wanted me to beg for his friendship, to plead with him. But, y'know, screw that. I had done nothing wrong.

I stood next to him. "Big weekend tent sale," I said.

Reynolds stared at the street. He said something that sounded like "dick."

"It's really stupid of you to blame me for what Gil did. It doesn't help to blame Gil either. He's a creep. We both know that."

Reynolds shifted his weight to his other foot. "I need something in my life, Becky. Gil is salt in the wound, you follow? Sometimes I want to quit this place. But the sick thing is, this is all I got right now. I need a little 'atta boy, Reynolds.' That's all. I'm caught in this shitty losing streak. I don't know what to do to snap out of it."

"Yeah," I said. "It's like there's a lot of money that flows through this place. Lots of opportunity. But it never seems to go our way, does it?"

We stood and contemplated the traffic.

"Things go in cycles," I offered. "Sometimes we just have to feel whatever shitty feelings we're feeling. From that will come the inspiration or insight to change everything."

I was talking out my ass, of course, but I wanted him to know that I cared. "We friends again?"

"See, now that's the thing I don't get, Becky," Reynolds shook his head. "You're this perceptive, interesting chick with an edge, with that whole lesbian thing going for you. You're so *cool*, but then you turn around and sleep with Gil."

"Did he tell you that? Reynolds, that's bullshit."

"Yeah, see. Women go for that kind of guy."

"Get over it, Reynolds. It's a lie."

"There's two kinds of guys. Nice guys and shitty guys. Women like the shitty guys."

"Reynolds, what makes you think you're such a nice guy?"

He looked at me, stunned. "Because I have *feelings*."

"Everyone has feelings."

"He clutched at his heart. But I know what it's like to really *hurt*."

His girlfriend had dumped him and kicked him out of her condo. That's why he was living in a van on the lot. Blah blah blah.

"Just because you got dumped doesn't mean you're a nice guy. It's not a Good Housekeeping seal of approval."

"I gotta find a woman who doesn't have a problem with men."

"Yeah, there's your life-changing answer." I exhaled hard.

"Hey, I thought we were friends again. Don't be pissed."

"Then be my friend, Reynolds. Don't try to make me into your girlfriend. Don't insinuate that I am — or should be — interested in men, interested in *you*. It's never going to happen."

"I'm your friend, Becky." He gripped my shoulders. "I'll watch myself. I promise."

"Incoming. He's mine." I walked toward the curb.

Squatty was right about the tent sale; there were so many Ups, all looking for a steal. I stopped caring about them. I just wanted to push them through the box and out the door. I got two-and-a-half deals, my personal best. But there were no cash spiffs — only a flat fifty bucks per deal. Squatty says it makes no sense to reward salesmen during a sale since a sale sells itself. But he gave Gil an expensive-looking wristwatch for being High Man, the salesperson with the most deals that day.

When I got home, I peeled off my shoes to see how bad the blisters were. Above the heel on each foot the blisters had broken, leaving raw scrapes. And my toes ached, but I could see no sign of blisters there. I wondered if I had enough bandages on hand to encase my feet in protective gauze and plastic for tomorrow's Day Two of the Carnival of Cars Big Top Blowout.

I filled a plastic lettuce crisper—the biggest container I could find—with cold water and ice cubes. I sat on my futon, closed my dust-rasped eyes and soaked my feet. I had time to breathe one full breath in and out before the phone rang. It was probably my mom wanting to hear all about my unique, extraordinary life.

"Becky? It's Linnie. How have you been?"

"Fine," I said, my eyes wide.

"What are you doing?" she asked.

"Soaking my feet in a salad bowl."

"I mean, what are you doing tonight?"

"No plans."

"Do you want to go to The Well?"

If I hadn't been so exhausted, I would've jumped at the invitation. "I'd love to, Lin, but I can't even limp. My feet are trashed."

"I'd like to see you." A moment of silence passed. "I could give you a foot massage."

"I couldn't ask you to do that," I said. "You're welcome to come over, uh, if you're comfortable with that. I'm just not very peppy." But all of a sudden, I *was* very peppy.

"Great," she said. "I'll drop by."

"Great." I gave her my address. Happiness surged through me. But as I hung up the phone, the words "I'll drop by" became a puzzling torment. "Drop by" made it sound like a pit stop. Did she mean that she was going to The Well without me, and since she would be in my neighborhood anyway, she'd drop by to say hello, then spend the rest of the night being hit on by lipstick lesbians? I pictured several lesbians flinging themselves against a brick wall. Queer girl makes a play for straight girl, queer girl gets hurt. Did Linnie really want to see me, or did she just want to go to The Well?

Either way, she'd be at my door in half an hour. The good thing about living in a studio apartment is that when there's tidying to be done, there's not a lot of square footage to contend with.

"You look tired," Lin said when I opened the door. She was holding a bottle of champagne and a freezer bag.

I ushered her in. "Sorry."

"I meant it in a sympathetic way."

"Hmm. Thanks." I hobbled back to the futon.

"I brought you chocolate ice cream." She went into the kitchen. "And caviar, because you said you liked it."

I had made a passing comment at dinner. I was surprised that she took note. "You brought me Fudge Caviar Ripple?"

"When you put it that way, it sounds nasty. But there's

champagne too. You're really going to like this kind. Where do you keep your crystal?"

"Lin, all my elegant stemware is imaginary at this point. Sorry. There are empty jelly jars in the second cupboard." I heard her open the cupboard. I listened for a murmur of disappointment. I didn't hear one.

"I like the heft of this glass," Lin said. I heard her unwrap the foil from the neck of the champagne bottle. Then I heard a low pop. "I never spill a drop. You're going to like this kind."

"Do you want music?" I asked, dragging myself to my iPod dock. "I'm in the mood for Lloyd Cole."

"Who's Lloyd Cole?"

"He's like a Scottish Leonard Cohen."

"Who's Leonard Cohen?"

"Linnie, Linnie," I said. I rose to the thrill of sharing my genius poet heroes with her. But there was a danger. What if she's indifferent to songs I love? I selected my favorite Lloyd Cole and Leonard Cohen random playlist. *Total exposure. Maximum emotional nakedness.* Let the chips fall where they may.

"You could light those candles," she said. "There's glare coming from that lamp."

"OK," I said. "Sorry."

"Can I tell you something about you that I've noticed?" Lin asked. I heard her open the silverware drawer.

"I don't really have silverware either. Sorry."

"That's what I was going to say, Becky. You're apologizing all the time. You don't need to apologize about things. Let people *deal*. It's not your responsibility how they feel." She came toward me with a jelly jar full of glittering champagne. "You seem tense. Sit down and relax."

I took the glass. "OK."

She went back into the kitchen. "I'm going to do your feet in a minute. I'm still a licensed cosmetologist. Can you believe that? I used to give pedicures to the Los Angeles Lakers. I bet you wouldn't have guessed."

"No, I never would've guessed," I said, watching the bubbles rise in my glass.

"I met tons of celebrities when I was doing pedicures," Lin said. "It's a glamorous job in that regard. But it's also the shittiest job in LA. Yeah, you're meeting all these famous people, but you're scraping their feet and cleaning the crap out from under their toenails. That's how I met Samuel."

"Scraping his bunions?" I asked.

Linnie laughed. "He doesn't have bunions. He told me that I was too beautiful to be at people's feet all day. He said he wanted to be at my feet."

"And that worked for you?" I asked.

"It was very romantic at the time," she said. "Samuel has always wanted to give me opportunities to better myself. He's passionately intellectual. He said that I should have a mind to match my beauty. Isn't that sweet? He insists on supporting me while I go to school."

"Sounds very *My Fair Lady*," I said. "In the most

patronizing sense." Linnie didn't respond. "Sorry," I said, "no offense."

Lin arranged a couple of bowls and plastic spoons on the coffee table — which was actually an upside down crate — along with the champagne bottle. "When you say sorry, Becky, it's like you're apologizing for taking up space on the planet. As if you're worried that you're inconveniencing others because of your existence. You need to get over that. You have a right and an obligation to take up space and be who you are." She sat down in the chair opposite me. "But you already know it. I can tell. You know better than I do." She raised her glass. "Here's a toast to…."

"To you and Samuel," I said, instantly regretting it.

"Here's to *enlightened carnality*," she said. She sipped from her jelly jar. "It tastes like sweet toasted sunlight, doesn't it?"

"It's very good."

"You like it?"

"Yes, Lin, I do. Thanks for bringing all this."

"It's not exactly dinner, but it's fun."

"What do you mean by *enlightened carnality*?"

"I'm still formulating my thesis." She ate a spoonful of ice cream. "A lot of people rebel against what they perceive as the social strictures regarding sexuality. I'm not so concerned about the constraints that other people place on me. I'm more fascinated by the constraints I place on myself. There are things that I want to do but won't allow myself—not because it's wrong, but because I'm afraid." She tasted the caviar. "There are things I feel that I won't even allow myself to fully feel. Know what I mean?"

"I'm not sure." I thought about it. Leonard Cohen sang a eulogy in the background. "You can't really control how you feel, can you? I guess you can suppress a feeling or decline to act on it, but that doesn't do much to change it," I said.

She nodded and took another drink. "Enlightened carnality is sexuality that transcends guilt and fear, but is also responsible and respectful toward others. That's how I picture it, anyway."

"Sounds good to me."

"So what happened to your feet?" She seemed eager to change the subject.

"Tent sale," I said. "I walked ten thousand miles today." I tried some caviar on a plastic spoon. "This is great."

"Sevruga."

I rolled it around in my mouth, then ate a chocolate ice cream chaser. Sweet, salty, odd flavor. "Lin, are you pregnant or something?"

Linnie chuckled. "As if."

I chose to read volumes of encouragement and promise into those two words. *As if.*

She sat on the floor in front of me and put one of my feet on her lap. "When I'm through, you'll want to go dancing with me. Sit back. You're all tensed up." She smiled. "Becky, close your eyes. *Relax.*"

I must have been staring bug-eyed at her. I couldn't believe that she was here using words like *carnality*, and that her warm hands were caressing my feet. I leaned my head back.

"I haven't done feet in a while," Linnie said. "I'm a professional student. I don't have a doctorate but I can hold my own in a conversation with Samuel and his friends. Right now, I'm taking History of Film, Art Criticism and a cooking class called Surprising Summer Salads. That's my favorite of the three. Samuel doesn't know I'm enrolled in that one."

"No offense, Lin, but Samuel sounds like a snob."

She was quiet for a moment as she massaged my toes. "Just because a person is educated doesn't mean that he or she is capable of self-examination." She pressed into the arch of my foot.

I closed my eyes. I'm pretty sure that I fell asleep at some point, because the next thing I heard was a Lloyd Cole song. Linnie was working on the sole of my other foot. I opened my eyes just a tiny bit, then a bit more.

"You are really beautiful, Lin."

"You just now noticed?"

"I noticed when I met you. But I didn't want to admit it. I didn't want to give you that emotional advantage."

"Becky, you don't even know how beautiful you are." She put my foot down. "How do you feel?"

"Great," I said. Wide awake.

"Let's go out."

Like a saintly nurse, Linnie dressed my wounded feet and we walked down Santa Monica Boulevard. People flowed in and out of the clubs. Throbbing dance music spilled into the air and mingled with the aroma of warm pavement and perfume. Neon signs. Cruising headlights. A rush of motion and desire.

Motorcycles — an impressive, gleaming row — were parked outside The Well. Linnie glanced at them. "Must be dyke night," she said with disdain.

"Hey, I'm a dyke," I said.

"Don't say that. You are not a *dyke*." She grabbed my elbow and pulled me through the door.

Was she joking, or was her dyke comment a hint of profound internalized homophobia lurking in her Florence Nightingale soul? A wall of noise inside The Well drowned out my thoughts.

Over the bar, video monitors flickered with images of women wrestling in body lotion. Tough-looking women dominated the two pool tables. I wished I could look tough. I tried to sneer but I'm afraid I looked like a bad Elvis impersonator. We moved to the bar and snagged beers, then we threaded through the crowd to the edge of the dance floor.

A new song pounded out of the speakers. Linnie whooped. "Let's dance!"

"I don't think my feet can take it," I said.

A brunette took Linnie's hand. "I'll dance with you."

As she was being pulled onto the dance floor, Lin gave me her beer.

"Go ahead," I shouted. I watched her dance for a few minutes. Then I jostled back through the crowd to observe the action at the pool tables. I leaned against a wall and fixed my gaze on green felt, pool sticks and clacking confetti-colored blurs.

Someone nudged me. "Hey. You wanna dance?"

I turned and met the eyes of a woman who could've passed for a teenage boy. Her hair was prickly blonde, buzzed short. She wore a faded flannel shirt and tattered blue jeans. Three metal studs in one earlobe. Unsmiling.

"I can't. I'm babysitting a beer."

"Did you drive?" she asked. She saw my blank expression and clarified, "I mean, do you have to drive home tonight?"

"No."

"Good." She led me toward the bar. "I wanna buy you a drink." Her tone was firm. "Two fuzzy tits," she told the bartender. "It's peach schnapps, cream and vodka. I just discovered it. It's my new favorite thing. So I want to share." She smiled. "This will kick your ass."

"Thanks, but I prefer beer. Just plain old beer, thanks."

Before I could graciously retreat in horror, the bartender slid two brandy snifters in front of us.

"Jeez, just try it. Live a little."

Grudgingly, I took a sip. "I guess there's alcohol in it,

right? I mean, you can't even taste it."

"Exactly. My name's Karen."

"Becky."

"Once you start drinking these, you can't go back to beer tonight," she cautioned. "You'll puke really ugly."

"Usually I puke so beautifully."

"Ha," she said. "I bet you do."

Karen was from Detroit. She told me about her mom, who was also a lesbian. They used to go out to bars together to meet women. "My mom and I have similar tastes," she said.

I thought about my mom and how hard it was for us just to shop for *clothes* together, let alone cruise chicks.

A couple of months ago Karen's mom flew in from Detroit for a visit. She stayed with Karen. Her mom ended up having an affair with Karen's lover. "It caused kind of a rift," she said. "They both live in Detroit now."

As Karen talked, I noticed things about her. A ready smile. A good sense of humor.

I could be attracted to her, I supposed. She is not, however, womanly. She is not more beautiful than Lin. How could anyone be more beautiful than Lin? Plus, Lin thinks I'm beautiful too.

I felt sadness crash inside me like a huge wave breaking along Will Rogers State Beach on a gray, windy day as a seagull flies overhead and craps on me. *Samuel.* Damn Samuel.

"Shit!" Linnie breathed. Her face glistened with light perspiration. "Which beer is mine?"

I pointed.

She chugged it down. "We gotta go. That woman—the one I danced with. She's all over me."

"This is my friend Karen."

Linnie looked at Karen. Then she looked back at me. "I really would like to leave now."

"Nice meeting you, too, blondie." Karen walked toward the pool tables.

"Hey, Karen," I said as Linnie pulled me toward the door. "Thanks for the fuzzy tit."

The air outside smelled like wood smoke and garlic wafting down from the Italian restaurant.

"Are you nuts?" Linnie hissed. "What did you do with her tits?"

"Lin, she was just being nice."

"She's stone butch, Becky. Bad energy."

"Why are you freaking out? What's stone butch?"

"I dance for two minutes and the next thing I know you're talking about some woman's tits."

"Why are you so pissed off?"

We walked a few paces.

"Why can't I just go dancing and not have it mean anything? Why do all you lesbians insist that I must be a lesbian too?"

"All you lesbians?" I asked. "Wait a minute, Lin."

We stopped.

"I'm confused about something here. You come to my place tonight, y'know, with champagne and caviar and there's candlelight and you're massaging my feet."

"Don't make a federal case out of it."

"It was very romantic by any standard."

"Becky, I can't be responsible for your perceptions or misinterpretations."

"Come on, Lin. Why are you being so defensive? It's OK to be curious."

"That's what I can't stand. You lesbians think that every woman is curious. You think we're all dying for a chance to sleep with another woman. I have plenty of opportunities, Becky. That woman was all over me tonight. I don't have to go to great lengths to seduce you. I'm not interested, OK?"

She was in my face, but she pulled back a little when she saw how she had stung me. Her voice was calmer, "I'm not interested in you that way. It's never going to happen. OK?"

I wanted to say, *Liar.* But I said, "Lin, I respect that. I respect you. We got our wires crossed. I've had a long day. I think we're on the same page now."

We both started walking again.

"I'm sorry I accused you," Lin said. "I've had a long day too."

We walked the rest of the way in silence.

My mind was reeling. How had such a perfect evening

gone so wrong? Was she jealous that I was talking to Karen? Was she mad at the woman she was dancing with, and taking it out on me? I figured that the last thing she wanted to hear me say was *sorry*.

She unlocked her car, which was parked in front of my building. "Thanks for going out with me, Beck," she said.

"Thanks for everything, Lin."

"Night." She ducked into her car without looking at me.

As I watched her drive away, I thought: *She's not trying to keep me away from her. She's trying to keep herself away from me.*

Whether this intuition was true, I don't know. But it felt as real as the memory of her touch on my battered and now throbbing feet.

Saturday morning marked Day Two of my bell-to-bell Carnival-of-Cars weekend, which entailed working from eight in the morning until nine at night.

In the freshly polished showroom floor I observed my reflection and, especially, the dark circles under my eyes. The vending machine squirted my coffee into a paper cup. Each cup was printed with five playing cards. Each time you got a cup of coffee, you were dealt a hand of poker. I examined my cup. Three sevens, two kings. Full house.

Reynolds came in, whistling. He looked as if he had just showered under the JetSpray car wash out back. A towel hung around his neck. "This is my day, Becky, I tell ya." He dropped coins into the slot. The coffee machine thumped and spat. He extracted his cup and studied it. "Four ladies," he said. "Queens beat a full house." He rubbed the towel on the side of his head, draining water from his ear. "Did you see the ad? It says: *Southland Auto Acres. Big Top Blow Out.*"

"Yeah. That ought to draw an upscale crowd." Coffee boiled in my stomach.

"Listen to the elitist college girl." Reynolds rested a hand on my shoulder. "Y'know, I thought about it, Beck." He held his face close to mine, insisting that I look into his eyes. "I was pressuring you yesterday. I'm sorry."

He smelled like car wax. A wave of nausea swept over me. "Forget about it."

He slid his thumb above my collarbone and massaged my neck. "You act all cool but I saw it."

"Saw what?"

"That *emotion*. My friendship means a lot to you."

"I'm not feeling well." I pulled away from him. "I didn't get much sleep."

He grinned. "Were you tossing and turning all night? Thinking about our fight? Thinking about the boy from the wrong side of the tracks?"

I glowered at him from under heavy eyelids. "Reynolds, how is it possible? How are you able to misread me so ridiculously?"

He slurped his coffee. "Why do you have to act like such a damn mystery?"

I fled through the big glass doors. The morning air tasted

sweet but it would soon be laden with traffic dust. I spotted Gil out on the lot. He was memorizing the inventory. He always knows which cars with what extras are parked where. His success isn't attributable solely to his talent for manipulating people. He knows his product.

The sun was still low in the sky. I held my hot, acrid beverage with both hands. Would Linnie call me today? Of course she would. But what would I say to her?

"Hey, Becky."

I saw Gil standing near Sweet Dream.

"I'm gonna sell this car today," he shouted. "So plan on having dinner with me."

I remained expressionless.

"You'll see."

Perhaps I could learn something from Gil, abhorrent though he was. He did not seem to take it personally that I rejected him. He was confident, playful even, especially compared to Reynolds. I felt zero attraction toward Reynolds, yet he assumed that I was expressing *emotion* toward him. Gil, on the other hand, merely insisted that he was a hot stud, and really, deep down, every woman wanted him.

Maybe I should adopt a Gil-like approach toward Linnie—give off a vibe of calm confidence as a dramatic foil to her confusion or conflictedness or whatever it is she's going through. She's crazy about me, after all. So isn't it inevitable that we will end up together somehow?

Linnie and me. A sure thing. No question.

Customer traffic on the lot had been heavy all day, but Reynolds was the only salesperson to score deals. Even Gil was in a slump. Early in the evening, when Ups became scarce, I thought about slipping into the back office to check my voice mail. I couldn't wait to hear the message from Linnie. At the same time, I felt vague dread.

I daydreamed about meeting Linnie for coffee at Urth Caffe where they make Spanish lattes — espresso with condensed milk. It's like a pudding more than a coffee, a bowl of sweet molten fat. Then we'd walk down the street and browse the shelves at the Bodhi Tree bookstore. Smoke from sandalwood incense would curl around us and Buddhist chants would echo hypnotically. She'd laugh at the life predicted for her in an astrology manual. I'd buy her a book of poetry, something to unravel the knots in her heart and set her free. Outside on the moonlit street, she would read a single verse of this miracle elixir poetry and she'd understand everything. She'd look at me, and for the first time we both would truly *see*.

"Hey gorgeous." Gil circled me, appraising. "As I see it, the problem is that lesbians have just never been with the right man."

"Gil, most lesbians have never even been with the right woman."

Reynolds walked past us, escorting another Up into the box.

"Reynolds is raking 'em in and I got bupkiss," Gil said. "Seriously, Beck. Forget all your politically correct crap. What about going and getting a beer with me after the bell?" He wrinkled his forehead in a pleading way.

"You look like Reynolds when you do that."

"I'll accept your pity." He interlocked his fingers and outstretched his arms, cracking his knuckles with a snap of his wrists. "I need sex." He laughed as if dismayed by his sudden, inexplicable lack of sex. "Having sex. Selling a car. It's all the same thing. Today has been an unmitigated fucking famine." He straightened his tie.

"I'm gonna follow up on a phone pop," I lied. I went inside to check my messages.

Linnie hadn't called. I held my head in my hands and stared at the phone. The reservoir of confidence that I had been building all day evaporated. What did it mean?

"You're looking at High Man!"

Reynolds stood in the doorway with a wide grin. He waved a slip of paper at me. "Squatty spiffed me dinner for two at that place on Sunset. That swanky place. You wanna go?"

"Now?"

"After I finish this deal." He headed for the box. "I had a realization today," he said. "Like a thunderbolt. I'll tell you about it tonight."

I hadn't said yes to dinner, but I knew that in Reynolds' mind we had a date.

Reynolds' hand was pressed against the small of my back

as the *maitre d'* led us to our table. Conversation eddied around us. I didn't like Reynolds touching me. I thought about jabbing my elbow into his ribs, but he was walking on air, and I thought it would be mean to smack him back to reality.

At the table, Reynolds beamed. "Don't you love it?"

I took a drink of ice water. The sharp coldness of it stung my teeth and spread into a dull ache at the base of my skull.

"A drink to start?" The waiter asked.

"Oh." Reynolds seemed overwhelmed by the prospect of having whatever he wished.

"Kir royal, please," I said.

"For me too," Reynolds smiled.

"What's a kir royal?"

"Champagne and cassis."

"What's cassis?"

"Just drink it when it comes."

"Kir royal. Sheesh. How do you know this shit?"

I held up the menu to deflect his admiring gaze. "What're you gonna have?"

"I'm thinking steak and maybe a lobster. Do they have curly fries?"

"I'm sure you can ask."

So we ate, and we drank a bottle of wine between us. Most of our discussion centered on The Fun Things

Reynolds Used To Do in High School. I listened absently and laughed whenever he seemed to want me to.

Partly, I felt bad that I was such a lousy dinner companion. Annoying though he was, Reynolds deserved to share his triumphant meal with someone who at least gave a rip.

I did give a rip, on some level, I suppose. But I was consumed with thoughts of Linnie. I can't even call them thoughts — they were more like impressions, all of them portents of doom.

Don't be silly, I told myself. *Don't take this to the moon. She'll call tomorrow. Or the next day. Give her time. Don't worry.*

I studied Reynolds' face, his rough-looking skin, large pores, shadow of beard, coarse tangled brows, reddish brown freckles on his nose and cheeks. His eyes were green. I never really took note of his eyes before. They were his best feature.

Yet compared to Linnie's arctic blues, Reynolds' eyes looked dull and irritated.

What does Samuel look like? What does Linnie see when she looks at him? Does she see eyes alive with possibility? Does she see a mouth that she wants to taste? Does she see what I see when I look at her?

The waiter cleared the table. Reynolds and I ordered coffee and chocolate cake.

"I haven't told you about my realization." He leaned toward me as if I'd been disguising my curiosity all evening.

"Your thunderbolt?"

"Right." He wiped his mouth with his napkin. "I know

why you never liked me—I mean liked me in a sexy way. I don't blame you. But everything's changed."

I had my own realization. There's no such thing as a free dinner. "Changed? How so?"

He leaned back in his chair. "So I'm out on the lot and I'm steamed about what you said to me this morning."

What had I said? "That you misread me so ridiculously?"

He nodded. "I was pissed off to the point where I didn't even give a crap about you. Where I just wanted to sell ten cars and to hell with you." He hastened to add, "Not that I feel that way about you right now."

"That was your realization?"

"Confidence," he said. "I quit caring about you and started caring about me. Just like Squatty tells us. It worked."

"So how have things changed between you and me?"

"I learned," he said. "It doesn't matter what you want from me. The important thing is what I want from you. I can get what I want if I'm willing to put myself out there, you know. With confidence."

What he said made sense in a cockeyed way. I had considered adopting a similar attitude toward Linnie. I needed to "put myself out there" with confidence. I needed to tell Linnie how I felt. I needed to do it immediately.

The waiter slid cake in front of us. The heavy, sweet smell of the frosting made my stomach lurch. I felt my dinner welling up from the pit of my stomach. How horrible it would be, I thought, if I were to drench Reynolds with vomit.

"I feel ill," I said. I felt intense urgency in my gut. "I have to go." I felt bad for abandoning Reynolds, but I couldn't sit there for another moment.

"Becky?"

I pushed away from the table.

"Where are you going?" Reynolds' voice faded.

I emerged onto Sunset Boulevard, gulped the air, and tasted its warmth and soot. I walked, then ran. Pain stabbed my feet with every step. Toward Linnie.

chapter **FOUR**

I planned to present myself at Linnie's front door and declare my passionate interest, Samuel be damned. I would put myself *out there*. My confidence and determination would inspire Linnie and would awaken her true longings. We would embrace. We would be together, always, always.

The most immediate obstacle to this plan was the fact that I did not know where Linnie lived. I remembered Marta mentioning that Linnie and Samuel lived near her. I toyed with the idea of canvassing several city blocks while shouting her name, despite my compromised feet. Ultimately, I decided that the best course of action would be to ask Marta where to find Linnie. Maybe I would even confess my feelings to Marta. Maybe I'd receive some sage advice in return.

I stood on the street in front of Marta's house. The thought of having to speak to Joy gave me pause. Joy's voice echoed in my memory: *Linnie is straight*. I could almost feel Joy squeezing my leg with sudden, bizarre force. I didn't want Joy to know anything about my feelings for Lin. But how could I talk to Marta without Joy knowing?

Through sheer curtains, I could see into Marta's living room. I expected to see Joy sitting on the sofa knitting feverishly like a spider spinning a web. But Joy wasn't there. Neither was Cyril.

I didn't want to ring the bell and risk the possibility

that Joy might answer. A far more reasonable and rational approach, I concluded, would be to peek into a few windows to see if Marta was at home.

I slinked between two bushes and into the back yard. All of the windows were dark. I saw a faint glow at the very back of the house.

As I passed a rosebush, a thorn snagged my skirt. I heard the whispery rip of fabric. A thorny cane from another rosebush bit my shin with a dozen tiny teeth, shredding my hosiery. I slid close to the French doors at the back of the house. I peered in from an angle. Candlelight flickered in the bedroom.

I heard voices, muffled. I sank to a crouch, cramping myself into the small space between the bushes and the wall. I tried to hear what was being said, but the voices were too low.

After an eternity of crouching, my feet were numb. My knees ached. Thorns rasped.

This is idiotic. What am I doing? The last thing I want to see is Marta and Joy having sex. Besides, what if they were to see me out here? How could I explain? They'd call the police.

I imagined being blinded by a flashlight beam, nudged by a nightstick, handcuffed and thrown into a patrol car. *We got her prints on file. She's a car salesman. Lock her up.*

The muscles in my legs had fallen asleep. The only way for me to extricate myself would be to lean forward and push up off the ground with my hands. I stretched. Pain shot from my hips to my ankles. I looked in the window. I had a clear view of the bed. A clear view of two nude bodies entwined: Marta and Linnie.

I sprang as if scalded, back through the bushes, toward the street. Tightness gripped my throat.

I felt as if a cherry bomb had exploded in my lungs. I just wanted go home, collapse into sleep and wake to find myself back in Denver, back in my parents' house, back in my old, small life with no horizons, no hopes, no disappointments. I walked as fast as my feet would allow.

My apartment building came into view. A man stood near my window, trying to peer through the blinds. It was Reynolds.

"What are you doing, Reynolds?"

He turned, mouth open. His expression seemed to glaze with acknowledgement that he had been caught doing something stupid.

"I wanted to make sure you were OK."

"That's why you're spying on me?"

"I'm not spying."

"Did you ring the bell?"

He shrugged. "No."

"Then you're spying on me."

He raised his hands, asking me to lower my voice. "You run out of a restaurant like that? I think I have a reason to check on you."

"I can take care of myself."

He noticed my shredded hosiery and thorn-scratched hands. "You don't look like it."

"Yeah, well." I surveyed the damage. I looked like I had been attacked by feral cats. "I'm fine now. Thanks for caring."

I was hoping that he'd shrug and mumble and go home. But he just stood there, staring at me, his head cocked to one side. The glow from the streetlamp illuminated his face in a sympathetic way.

"Becky, can we go inside and talk?"

"Reynolds, I am not interested in you. Do us both a favor and forget me, OK?" I opened the door to the lobby of my building. "It's never going to happen with us." I looked into his wide, wounded eyes. "Give it up, Reynolds. It's never ever going to *fucking* happen." I shut the door on him and didn't look back.

I couldn't sleep and couldn't cry. I stared at the ceiling until my alarm clock buzzed. It was an uneven tone, a pulsing and rhythmic series of shorter buzzes merging into one long buzz. I listened to it for several minutes before I switched it off. As I showered, I watched the water dance on my skin. I breathed the steam. I closed my eyes and turned my face to the full spray. In my mind I saw the indelible image from last night: Linnie and Marta, together, nude, making love on the bed.

It was none of my business. It had nothing to do with me. I was not intended to witness it. But I couldn't help wondering: How long had their affair been going on?

More important, why was Linnie with Marta instead of me?

Reynolds did not show up for work in the morning. Squatty went to the back lot and pounded on the van where Reynolds usually slept. There was no answer.

"All his gear is back there, but he ain't," Squatty said as he paced back and forth in front of me. "His car's gone." Squatty spat on the asphalt. "I used to spiff cash all the time. But then my High Man wouldn't show up for work the next day. I find out they'd been drinkin' and druggin' on the money I give 'em. So now I give 'em a nice dinner out or a wristwatch or tickets to a ballgame." He noticed the scratches on my hands and shins. "I hope that boy hasn't gone and done something foolish."

"He can take care of himself, Squatty," I said. "I'm sure he'll call."

"That would take a load of worry off my mind."

I felt like a shitbag. I had upset Reynolds. I had told him to fuck off at what was probably a very vulnerable moment for him. I was responsible for his absence.

Gil walked toward us. "What's the word on Reynolds?"

"AWOL," Squatty said. "He was on a streak. He coulda sold cars today." Squatty turned and headed toward the showroom. "Get busy and *sell*. You gotta make up for your missing crewmate."

Gil looked at me. "I'm serious, OK. This is no bullshit."

"What?"

"We have to work as a team. No skating. No sharking. If you have an Up that gets tough, turn him to me. I will split every deal with you. Promise me, OK? Do *not* let an Up walk off this lot unless he goes through me first. Got it?"

I studied him. "Reynolds and I trusted you before. You burned us every time."

"If I burn you this time, I swear, you can kick me in the balls." Gil looked serious. "We have to move a lot of product. Are you with me or against me?"

"Somewhat reluctantly, I'm with you."

Traffic was heavy. I dutifully turned my Ups to Gil. He was closing a lot of deals. We were both like machines. I discovered that it's easy to smile aggressively and glad-hand when you hate yourself.

I hated that I had hurt Reynolds. I hated that Linnie did not love me, did not care for me in the slightest. My intuition told me otherwise, though. Somehow I *knew* or felt that Linnie wanted me. She wanted to be with *me*, not Marta, not Samuel. I felt it solidly and certainly because of our chemistry. Chemistry can't be faked.

But what I hated the most was that in my deepest and most certain way of knowing I was dead wrong. I hated this the most: In my deepest and most certain way of knowing, I was *dead wrong*. My intuition was lying to me. I had seen proof of this lie last night on Marta's bed.

If I can't even trust my own gut feelings, whom can I trust? How did my capacity for self-deception become so immense?

All day on the lot I was haunted by hallucinations. They weren't genuine hallucinations, I suppose, just vivid imaginings. I imagined Linnie and Marta making love on the back seat of Sweet Dream, for example. I did note with some satisfaction, however, that Gil had been unable to sell that car.

The movie of Linnie and Marta together kept playing in my mind. I felt excluded yet included at the same time. They looked beautiful together, irresistible. What I had seen the night before was so intimate that I felt almost like a participant. Yet I was horrified to have been literally on the outside looking in.

I felt like an adolescent, as if everyone in the world understood love and relationships except me. I wondered if I had missed a crucial phase of my emotional development. I never had the chance to be a silly puppy-loving teenager. When I was in high school, I just assumed that my romantic impulses were all wrong, so I suppressed them. As far as I was concerned, romance didn't apply to me. If I had acknowledged my feelings for women back then, would I have a better understanding of romantic relationships as an adult?

Later in the day, I pictured Linnie with a man whom I imagined to be Samuel. Actually, he looked exactly like Gil. He picked up Lin in his arms and twirled her. They laughed hollowly.

The more I imagined Linnie with this Gil/Samuel hybrid, the more hurt I was. *Linnie led me on, only to snub me. What a bitch.*

Were Lin and Samuel still together? Did Samuel know

about the affair? Did Joy? And what about Reynolds, conspicuous in his absence?

Reynolds and I were similar. Both of us were chasing women we didn't understand. We were both trying to wring love out of people unlikely to reciprocate our desire. We were both unwilling to heed the most obvious clues. We were pitiful.

I must've looked heartsick because Squatty jogged up to me in his waddling sort of way. "Love is like water, Becky," he said. "It takes the form of the container that holds it." He paused to catch his breath. "Say you got a kidney-shaped swimming pool. Fill it with water and you got kidney-shaped water. Same with love."

"I'm not sure I follow you," I said.

"It's like rain," he said. "Love is like rain. When it rains, it rains on everyone just the same. But different people have different capacities. People will say that there are all kinds of love—parental love, romance. That ain't true. There is just the one thing called love. People have their various capacities and ways of channeling it. Different expressions are appropriate for different situations, which is why there seems to be so many kinds of love. Some folks have roots that suck up the water. Some bloom and grow. Some hold it all in like a cactus. Others just let the rain slide off. That's how it is, Becky. That's how it is with love."

I nodded to humor him. "Thanks, Squatty." I hoped that one day I would have a worldview that provided me with inspiring metaphors.

"If I may be frank," he said in a low voice, "sex ain't love."

He cleared his throat. "Now quit moping and sell some more cars," he said, waddling back to the showroom.

I found it disturbing that my innermost personal distress was visible to everyone within a hundred yards of me. *Does everyone know things about me that I don't know myself? Does everyone have advice for me?* I remembered what Linnie had said about Samuel, "Just because someone is educated doesn't mean that he or she is good at self-examination."

I was living my life, trying to give everyone a fair shake. But I couldn't see into people's hearts and understand their needs. I couldn't soothe their deepest agony—but I wanted to. Wasn't that presumptuous of me? All of the hurts and needs that I saw in other people were probably just projections of my own fuckedupness. Maybe I was the type who, instead of noticing that I'm on fire, insists that the air conditioning must be broken.

I needed to study myself, but not too hard. To examine too closely would be like looking at my skin under a magnifying glass; I'd find a weather-beaten landscape of unrelieved emptiness and wonder how the hell it pertains to me.

I looked at my reflection in the windshield of a car. What did I want or expect from my own life? I needed a manifesto.

I want to live a life that is truly and uniquely my own. I want to make choices and bear the full brunt of the consequences. I want to restrain myself from classifying those consequences as good or bad. I want to hear and see and think for myself, to consider others with respect but to not be bound by their opinions. I want to be free. Absolutely free.

That was the idea, anyway.

I had hoped that Reynolds would arrive later in the day, but he didn't. Squatty gave Gil a box of expensive cigars for selling the most cars. Together, Gil and I moved seven cars in one day. He finished ahead of me by half a deal, though, because he had closed a sale for a member of a different sales crew.

"Hot damn," Gil said, flashing the cigar box at me. "I'm good to my word, Beck. I'm splitting this with you fifty-fifty."

"Keep them," I said.

"I want you both here *promptly* at the bell tomorrow," Squatty said. "Don't pull a Reynolds on me." Squatty locked the showroom and got into his car.

"I'm gonna see if Reynolds is back yet," Gil said.

I was just about to say the same thing. I was curious if Reynolds had somehow slipped in without anyone noticing.

Gil and I walked toward the van in the back lot.

"Don't taunt him, Gil. Don't wave your spiff under his nose."

"Relax. I wanna share a smoke with the guy." We walked a few paces. "If you're good, I'll school you in the fine art of the smoke."

Reynolds' van was parked in the back lot under a fluorescent light with a bad bulb that dimmed and flickered at irregular intervals. I knocked on the van. No answer. I opened the back doors and was overpowered by the smell of pine-scented air freshener. The interior was empty except for a sleeping bag, a pillow, a pile of clothes and a cardboard box. I sat down on the bumper. Gil sat next to me.

"You realize that you've placed yourself in a compromising position," Gil said. "If I weren't a gentleman, I could take advantage of these circumstances."

I thought for a moment. He was right. "Yeah, you could rape me if you wanted to, if that's what you're saying."

"Whoa, whoa!"

"But you're not that kind of a guy, are you? You don't want to shove it down my throat, so to speak. You want me to buy it. You want me to drive off the lot grinning even though I just got screwed. That's because you're a salesman. I got no worries about you."

Actually, I was a little bit worried. I mentally rehearsed the rape-thwarting techniques I had learned in my sorority's self-defense class.

After a few minutes of staring out across the back lot, Gil rubbed his knuckle against his nose. "Don't take this as a compliment, but you're different, Beck. You're different than the women who go out with me."

"I should hope so." I tapped my foot nervously. "I thought you were gonna show me how to smoke a cigar."

Gil opened his box of cigars. "Watch and learn." He produced a cutting instrument from his jacket pocket and sliced the ends of two cigars. "Lick this," he said.

"No licking," I said.

He lit a match and turned the end of one cigar over the

flame. He puffed gently. He handed the cigar to me.

I hesitated. "That's been in your mouth."

"Jeez. Don't inhale. Just puff."

I took the cigar and did as he said. He lit the other.

We smoked in silence.

"See what I'm saying? That's a cigar." Gil kicked off his shoes. "Take off your shoes."

"If I do I won't be able to get them back on," I said. I felt lightheaded from the cigar. "This is a terrible buzz."

"It's an acquired taste."

I puffed again, trying to give it a chance. "So why don't you have a date tonight?"

He puffed. "Why don't you?"

"The woman I want to be with lives with a man, her boyfriend. She's also having an affair with the only woman I've ever slept with."

The fluorescent light above Reynolds' van went out. The ember of Gil's cigar glowed. "Seriously? That's very fucking complicated. I went out with a bisexual chick for a while. It's every guy's fantasy, right? But it was very fucking complicated. I never knew where I stood. I kept wondering, *Does she want to be with me or is she thinking about some chick?*"

"If you're saying that to make me think you're a sensitive guy with nuanced emotions, I'm not buying it."

Gil and I smoked. The fluorescent light came back on.

"Didn't you ever wonder what it's like to sleep with a guy?" Gil asked.

"What makes you think I haven't slept with a guy?"

"Educated guess. Like I said, you're *different*."

I thought about it. "Yeah. It would be interesting to see what it's like." *It would be interesting, maybe, to understand an aspect of Linnie's reality*. "Gil, did you ever think about sleeping with a guy just to understand your girlfriends' point of view? Seriously. You know, like a gender-role thing?"

"That's *insane*. That's almost sick, Becky. Guys don't do shit like that." He puffed his cigar. "See, I think that if you would just have sex with a guy just once, you'd be a happier person."

"But the same isn't true for you, sleeping with a guy just once," I said with a laugh. "OK, then." I stubbed out my cigar on the asphalt. "Let's go."

He looked at me, blank. "Where?"

"Let's do it. Let's fuck."

He smiled ruefully. "Ha haa, Becky. Not funny."

"So all of a sudden you're not so sure of yourself?" I climbed into the van. "Come on. Right here."

The fluorescent light went out again. Gil stood. "What about Reynolds?"

"I can't imagine that this will take very long." I opened the cardboard box and rooted through it, hoping to find— "Here." I held up a packaged condom. I flicked it at Gil as if it were a cigar butt. "Put this on."

Gil climbed into the van and closed the doors behind him. "You won't regret this, Becky. You won't regret it." He took off his jacket and hung it on the back of the driver seat. He slid his tie off and draped it over his jacket. "So you've never done this before?"

"In a custom-conversion van? No."

There was a tremor in Gil's voice, and a new urgency in his fiddling with the buttons on his shirt. "Becky, you're a virgin."

"Hardly."

"But you've never done this before, right?" On his knees, he shuffled closer to me as he unbuttoned his shirt. "So technically you are."

"Gil, it's hard for me to have sympathy for you. All you care about are meaningless technicalities regarding specific acts. You have no clue about the emotional complexity of intimacy, which doesn't necessarily require sexual contact. Once you've had your heart broken, you're no longer a virgin. That's the demarcation as far as I'm concerned."

"I know, I know. You're right. You're right." His breathing was heavy. "Tell me more about *intimacy*." He draped his shirt over his jacket and tie. His chest was broad and hairless. He put his hands on my hips and started nuzzling my neck.

He felt like sandpaper and spit. I pushed him away. "Let's be clear about this. I'm not attracted to you. I don't want your mouth to be anywhere near mine. I don't want to touch you more than I absolutely have to. I'd like to remain fully clothed."

He pulled away without protest. "So how do you want to do it?" He stretched out on Reynolds' sleeping bag. "I think you'll at least have to get rid of the pantyhose."

"Probably." I winced as I slipped my shoes off and flopped down next to him. "I'm viewing this as an exercise in bridge building." I wriggled out of my hosiery and panties. "I want to understand you and your people, the heterosexual lifestyle in general." I turned to look at him. "Do *not* get any fluids on me."

He propped himself on his elbow. "Since you're new at this, I think you should be on top."

"Agreed."

He reached out and stroked my cheek with the backs of his fingers. "This is great."

I pushed his hand away. "This is science."

He pressed his back to the floor and slid his pants off. "I think you're gonna enjoy this, Becky." He clasped his hands under his head and stretched out, nude.

This would be a good time for Reynolds to make a grand entrance, I thought.

I sat up and looked at Gil's body.

"Well?" Gil asked.

"Eh. You're a guy."

"You just now noticed?"

"I mean all guy bodies are pretty much the same."

"If you're saying I'm average, you don't know shit."

I picked up the condom packet and handed it to him. "As previously noted. I've never cared to examine guys."

He ripped open the packet. "Why don't you put this on me?"

"Show me how it's done, Superman."

He opened the packet. "Women should have to pass a class in basic romance, maybe as part of your home economics training." He fumbled around. "Don't be so combative. We're about to make love."

"We're about to fuck, Gil. I see a big difference." I straddled him.

"Do you know what to do?"

"Do you?"

With a push, he was inside me.

It hurt much less than I imagined it would. It didn't feel good or bad, it was just there.

We stared at each other for an awkward moment.

"What now?" I asked.

"Usually there's pleasure and grunting."

"That's not going to happen."

He wriggled. "You're doing it wrong. You act like you're not even into this."

"I'm a lesbian, Gil. What do you expect?"

He started to thrust. "How's that?"

"Tolerable."

I imagined being in Linnie's body instead of my own, trying to feel what she would feel with Samuel. I was overwhelmed with longing for her.

"You know what I love about a woman, Gil?"

"What?"

"Everything. The sound of her voice. The texture of her hair."

He thrust more quickly, more forcefully.

"The way she moves. The way she smells. *Breasts*, Gil. Embracing thighs."

A paroxysm. Then he relaxed. He closed his eyes. His whole body seemed to soften.

I was disappointed. "That's it?" I separated myself from him. "Is that all there is?"

His chest heaved for a moment. Then he looked at me and smiled. "You're a lesbian. What did you expect?"

I smiled back. "I told you."

We both started to laugh, self-consciously at first, then genuinely, then fading.

He reached for his pants. "Better get out before Reynolds shows up."

Poor Reynolds. "He'd be pissed if he knew about this." I wrestled with my hosiery.

"Becky, he just wants to bone you." Gil zipped his fly.

"Maybe, but he's my friend."

"He's your friend only because he wants to bone you."

"You wanted to bone me and you weren't my friend."

He buttoned his shirt. "Now I've boned you, and I'm still not your friend."

I pointed to the withered latex. "Get rid of that."

"Seriously, you don't owe Reynolds anything, Beck." He grabbed his jacket. "You don't owe me anything, either."

"What could I possibly owe you?"

He finished pulling himself together. "I don't know." He reached for his box of cigars. "Maybe a hug?"

I laughed, certain that he was kidding.

A shadow crossed his face, and I knew that he was serious. But without missing a beat, he winked. "Let's get outta here."

I opened the back doors, half expecting to see Reynolds standing there with wounded eyes.

Gil slammed the van doors. "See you tomorrow."

"Yeah," I said. "Tomorrow."

We walked to our cars.

"We were a great team today, Becky."

"Yeah, we were in a groove. See you tomorrow."

"Drive safe," he said. "Take care."

As I drove home I realized that the impossible — such as my having sex with Gil — was clearly possible, given the right circumstances. Maybe that's what happened with Linnie and Marta, a sudden convergence of propitious yet temporary circumstances. I wondered if Samuel was just like Gil — kind of an asshole, but kind of OK.

I can't claim that I gained any real insight from having sex with Gil. But I had succeeded in the horribly stupid and reckless task of screwing the most wrong person in my life. I felt that, somehow, I had gotten even with Linnie.

Late-morning sunlight fell in heavy bands across my bed. My arms were wrapped around my pillow. My hands were stiff, as if I'd spent the night clutching a lover who I feared would slip away from me.

I willed myself out of bed and went to the door to pick up my morning newspaper. I saw an envelope. Someone had pushed it under my door.

It was lavender and small. A love letter? From Linnie?

Or Reynolds?

Or *Gil*?

I tore it open. It read: Marta and Joy Request the Honor of Your Presence to Celebrate the Third Birthday of Our Precious Cyril.

On the back was written: *Becky, please come. Sorry for the short notice. Linnie.*

The party was that same night at eight, at Marta and Joy's house.

That morning I was late for work. Squatty didn't seem to mind. Reynolds was back, working an Up.

I got my coffee from the machine. I drew a straight. Just my luck, a *straight*. I stood on the outdoor platform.

Ultimately, Reynolds' Up walked without writing a deal. The woman kept smiling and apologizing to him as she got into her car. "Sorry, it just doesn't work for me," she said. "Thank you, though, for all your hard work."

That's the story of his life, I thought. He has probably heard those same words a million times. A rejection wrapped in a better-luck-next-time smile. Poor guy.

Then again, he was probably packing the numbers or saying idiotic shit, so she walked. Good for her.

Either way, I prepared myself to give him a pep talk and ask him where he had spent that past twenty-four hours.

He turned up his palms and shrugged at me. I waved him over. He hitched up his trousers. He looked as if he had lost five pounds.

"You dropped a lot of weight in a day," I said.

"My metabolism," he grinned. "I pissed it all outta me."

Lovely.

Gil swooped in. "Can't believe Squatty didn't shitcan you, Reynolds."

"Yeah." Reynolds was silent for a moment. "I told him my mom died."

"Oh, jeez, Reynolds." My heart went out to him. "When did you hear?"

He snickered. "About ten fuckin' years ago. I went to Vegas and lost my ass at the craps tables. That's where I was. I didn't have enough money for gas to get home."

"Don't joke about moms, man," Gil said.

"Why did you go to Vegas?" I asked.

Reynolds glanced at Gil. "A certain someone made me feel like a fucking loser. It really chapped my ass."

So, wanting to prove something, Reynolds drove to Vegas to parlay all his worldly cash—approximately five hundred dollars—into a fortune.

"I'd had such a shitty night," he said, referring to his time spent with me. "But, overall, I'd had a lucky day. Now or never, I said to myself. This could be the only day that Lady Luck smiles on Jack Reynolds."

So he went to Vegas and stood at a craps table for less than an hour.

"I was up two hundred, then down a bill, then up six. Then it was gone. All gone. I was flat busted broke with an empty gas tank. Turns out, my ex-girlfriend cancelled all my credit cards."

"Did you have to peddle your candy ass on the street?" Gil asked.

"So there I am in Vegas, without a pot to piss in. I wandered outside, not knowing what to fucking do next. I almost started to cry. I looked down the strip and all of a sudden I had a *vision*." Reynolds' face beamed. "I was a little misty-eyed, right," he said. "The whole strip is lit up like a million Christmas trees, like—you know what? You know what I remembered? This thing from when I was a kid."

He looked at Gil and me as if he expected us to blurt out the answer.

"The best fucking thing in my life! The Electric Light

Parade at Disneyland. It's like a zillion lights in every color. And there's this music, a synthesizer riff like a drug that makes you grin and stare and dance. All these cartoon images made of light dance in front of you. There's just nothing like it."

"So you were having an acid flash?" Gil asked.

Reynolds waved his arms as if trying to awaken in us the excitement he felt. "It was a *happiness* flash. I was standing there in Vegas with colored lights dancing all around me, and I remembered when I was a kid. How happy I felt, how free. I felt it all fresh. Dazzled by everything, y'know? So I thought, *jeez*, where did this happy shit come from? I'm a million miles from Disneyland and a zillion bucks in debt. The answer, you guys, the answer *blew me away*."

Gil looked almost sincerely interested. "What?"

"Inside. It came from *me*. That was my epiphany." Reynolds thrust his arms in the air like a football ref signaling a touchdown. "The happiness didn't come from the strip, or the lights. It didn't come from money or a girlfriend or any of that shit. No matter how shitty things get, no matter if I lose everything, I have happiness, you guys. He tapped his chest with a self-satisfied smile. *Right here*."

"Shit," Gil said. "I suppose you floated back to LA on a cloud."

"No." Reynolds raised his hand. "This is where it gets good. I walked up and down the strip, totally jazzed. I was, like, so happy I couldn't stand still. After a while, I got tired of walking. I sat down, took off my shoes and leaned against a wall. I'm there maybe two seconds when some lady walks by and drops three quarters in my shoe." Reynolds looked amazed. "It was a *sign*. So I poured the coins into my hand, put on my shoes and went into the nearest casino. I was on autopilot. I walked right up to this one slot machine as if it had said, Reynolds, get your ass over here. I fed it the quarters. I pulled the lever. What are the odds?" He shrugged in disbelief. "I won $38,769 on the progressive slots. But that's just gravy, you guys. The meat and potatoes, I'm telling you, is happiness." He strutted toward the curb. "Where's my next Up? Bring me a fuckin' Up."

Gil and I watched him, then looked at each other.

"I think he had a religious experience," I said.

"Yeah." Gil thought about it. "Maybe I had a religious experience too." He rubbed his nose with his knuckle. "I've seen the light. What happened last night between you and me was unwise, OK? It was a bad move on my part. I should have said no. OK?"

"It's no big deal, Gil. I wanted to try it."

"It *is* a big deal. You should've done it with a guy you like, a guy who is nice. Someone you care about, someone with values. Instead, you picked me. I'm a *shit*, Becky." He was earnest. "Promise you'll sleep with some guy other than me. Promise you'll find someone you can have a good experience with."

"Are you worried that you're going to lose your job as official spokesman for heterosexuality?" I teased. "Besides, I do care about you, Gil."

"Not like *that*," he said.

"I don't care about any guys like *that*."

"OK, then forget the whole thing," he said, bristling. "I'm sorry it wasn't better for you, that's all."

"It's not you, Gil. It's not guys." I tried to explain. "It's like — say you love the ballet. You want to go to the ballet, but someone takes you to the circus instead. How much fun can you expect to have?"

"Everyone loves the circus, Becky. No one likes ballet. That's a shitty analogy."

"All I'm saying is don't worry about it."

He shrugged. "Yeah." He shuffled his feet in a way that reminded me of Reynolds. "Maybe we should try it one more time, then. Just to be sure." I saw a hint of a smirk on his face.

"Jeez," I said, "You never quit. You already got what you wanted."

"Becky, I never quit because I never get what I want. Damn! Fucked up as this sounds, I want what he has," Gil said, jutting his chin toward Reynolds. "Nobody expects anything from him. He stumbles through life and it all works out. Look at him. He's free."

"I'm sure he doesn't feel that way most of the time," I said.

"Still. Lucky bastard."

I decided to wear faded Levis and a white T-shirt. That way I would look casual and slightly apathetic, as if the party were no big deal, as if I were going to a simple beer blast instead of the most crucial West Hollywood doggie fête of the decade.

Why would Linnie invite me? Why at the last minute?

I wanted to see her because I felt that we had some unresolved business between us. Maybe she felt the same way.

At the market down the street I looked at the wine selection. I thought about picking out a nice bottle of red. I pictured Joy taking it out of my hands and consigning it to the recycle bin.

I grabbed a six-pack of cheap beer. I chose a packet of imitation-meat dog snacks for Cyril and slapped a red cellophane bow on it.

Joy and Marta's house buzzed with women, all of whom looked unfamiliar to me. There was no sign of Linnie. I was the only person wearing jeans. Lesbo-generic music — acoustic-guitar anthems — wailed. A banner was plastered on the wall, *Happy Birthday, Cyril.* Arcs of crepe paper swung from the ceiling. An unnaturally tan woman in a silk pantsuit took my package of dog treats and tossed it onto a table filled with lavishly wrapped packages. Purple foil. Plump green bows. Festive spirals of yellow ribbon.

"The bar is in there." The woman waved toward the kitchen.

The eyes of two unimpressed women followed me as I went to get a drink. I felt as if I were back in high school; I didn't belong.

"Becky." Joy said my name as if she had caught me doing something illegal. She stood behind an arsenal of bottles arranged on the breakfast bar. She plucked a plastic cup from a stack and dropped a few ice cubes into it. "What'll you have?"

"Just a beer." I slid my six-pack onto the table. I scanned

the room for Linnie. "Where's Cyril?"

"With his mother somewhere." Joy splashed three or four different kinds of booze into the cup. "Here. My specialty." She held it out to me.

"Just a beer would be fine."

"It's a party, Becky. Enjoy." She made it sound like a threat.

I took a sip of the drink. It tasted like bug spray.

"Linnie was looking for you," Joy said. She motioned for me to come closer. "I think you have a chance with her," Joy whispered. "Go for it."

"Uh. Thanks."

I jostled my way down the hall, past the unsmiling women who were waiting for the bathroom. Why can't lesbians all be nice to one another? *Why can't we look one another in the eye and exchange smiles of comradeship?* I scowled at the women I passed.

"Becky." Linnie pressed herself against me. "You came." She seemed happy to see me. "I want to talk to you."

I was happy to see her, too, not just because she was smiling and familiar. She looked much prettier than I had remembered, although she had dark circles under her eyes. I smoothed her eyebrow with my thumb. She pulled away.

She led me into a room and closed the door.

I realized that we were standing in Marta and Joy's bedroom.

Linnie moved toward me as if she were going to kiss me.

"Don't do that." I stepped back.

"What's wrong?" Her eyes searched.

"That." I pointed to the bed. "Because of that. You and Marta are having an affair."

A fraction of a moment passed. "You're *hallucinating*." She said it so calmly that I wondered.

Was I hallucinating?

"I know what I saw," I said.

"What did you see?" Linnie's eyes hardened. "Saw? *How?*"

"God, Linnie, I'm sorry. It's all so stupid." I wanted to run away. "It's just that I…."

"You *what*? You saw something?" She was on the offensive now. "What did you see, Becky?"

"I wanted to be your girlfriend," I said. "I wanted to be with you."

We looked at each other for a moment. The hardness of her gaze was unbearable. I went for the door and found myself back in the hallway.

The crowd in the living room was singing Happy Birthday to Cyril. I heard Joy's voice at the top of the song. The women who had been waiting in line for the bathroom had moved into the living room.

Marta came around the corner. "There you are." She took my cup and drained it.

Marta pulled me into the bathroom and held me firmly by the hips. She pressed my back against the door and put her tongue in my mouth.

"What are you doing?" I pushed her away. "We need to talk."

"Do we have to?" She kissed my neck.

"This is *wrong*."

The doorknob rattled. Someone knocked. Was it Linnie?

"I'll take a rain check. Don't go far, Becky. I haven't forgotten how much fun we had that night." Marta swatted my ass. She opened the door and rejoined the party.

"Hey, Maaarta," said the woman in the hallway It wasn't Linnie after all. "Great paaarty."

Marta went into the bedroom where I assumed Linnie still was. I went in the opposite direction, toward the kitchen. Joy was at her station, mixing a drink. Women were chatting around platters of finger food.

I saw my six-pack of beer. I grabbed a bottle. It felt cold and solid in my hand, like an anchor to the real world. I twisted off the cap and took long pull. It tasted like, yes, pure Rocky Mountain spring water.

"Becky, I wish you would expand your horizons and have a real drink." Joy grabbed the beer bottle away from me. "Please don't drink that trailer-trash swill in my house."

I was angry with everyone—Marta, Linnie. Joy became the focus for my anger. "All I want is a beer, Joy."

She picked up a cup and a bottle of scotch. "This is a quality beverage, Becky. Watch and learn."

"A *beer*, Joy." My voice rose. "I want a plain pisswater beer from Colorado. You're a snob, Joy. You think you're arch and trendy but you're a fucking insecure loser clinging to your shitty, lying, cheating girlfriend."

She jutted her chin at me. "Don't *talk* trailer trash in my house either."

Joy hated me. She was outraged by Marta's infidelities. I knew that I was pulling the tail of a potentially vicious dog.

"You're so damn obtuse, Joy. You don't *see*. You don't hear."

Joy shoved me hard.

I shoved her back.

Other partygoers were electrified. "Violence is not the answer," one woman exclaimed. Another said, "Ladies, let's dialogue."

"I've heard enough," Joy said. She grabbed a fistful of my hair and spun me toward the door. "I'm calling the police."

"Marta is *fucking* every woman in LA, Joy! She fucked me! She fucked Linnie in your own damn bed," I shouted.

The open door. Fragrant evening air. A sharp jab in my back. The ground flew up at me. My nose pressed into the lawn.

Joy grabbed my shirt and flipped me over. I flailed. The back of my hand connected with her face.

"You don't know shit!" Joy kicked me. Again and again. "You don't know shit!"

Legs and bodies, backlit jagged shadows. My blood throbbed, drowning the voices that rallied impotently for peace. "Violence only begets violence. An eye for an eye makes the whole world blind."

Joy sat on my chest. My arms were pinned under her knees. Hands like rock closed over my throat.

I couldn't move, couldn't speak. I closed my eyes against everything. I smelled the fresh-cut grass. A smell of my childhood. Seven years old. Before Linnie. Before Marta. Long before any of this, I was seven years old, twirling on an emerald lawn in the long shadows of Denver summer. I would spin and spin, melting the houses and trees into a blur. I would hold my arms out from my sides, feeling my hands grow heavier as the world went by, faster and faster. Then I'd fall into the mossy tang of the grass. The ground would wobble. Houses would bounce into place. Trees would sway to a stop.

The world would be put right again.

The pressure on my neck disappeared. The weight on my chest lifted. I opened my eyes to the faces above me, twisted, pitying. I was sprawled, nauseated, soaked in my own tears.

"You *should* cry," Joy spat. "I should've killed you."

Marta was holding her back.

Joy kicked my shoe as if kicking the tire of a car. Marta coaxed her away from me, pulled her inside. Others moved back into the house.

A teardrop trickled into my ear as I gazed up at the quiet night. I looked for a constellation to orient me. But no stars were bright enough to shine through the haze and encompassing glare of the city.

"Are you OK?" It was Linnie's voice.

The grass felt damp under me. I rose to my feet. I backed away from her.

"Come here," she said softly.

"I never meant to make trouble for you, Linnie." I touched my burning neck. "Sorry," I said. "I'm sorry. Sorry."

She moved toward me. "Becky, are you all right?"

I burst into a run. Over the hedge, off the curb, down the middle of the street, I sprinted as if chased.

"Becky," Linnie yelled.

I imagined a hand, a woman's hand, one of Linnie's miraculous hands, fingers outstretched, almost caressing me, beckoning me to her.

I ran hard, farther and farther away from her.

Halfway home, I considered the possibility that I wasn't running away. I was running toward something—toward that feeling on the lawn, that seven-year-old freedom. I ran harder, lungs stinging. Faster. I felt blood, pain and power in every cell.

chapter **FIVE**

The morning after the party I awoke with a sense of relief, as if the worst had happened and I could glide through the rest of my life knowing that I had survived it. My aches were mild. Between the time I showered, dressed and got out the door, however, I developed a mood to match the purpling contusions that Joy had left on me. The clarity I felt while running home last night was now dull and muted. Everything seemed fuzzy.

I stood on the outdoor display platform as the morning sun flooded the showroom. I searched for some thought to hold onto. I remembered Linnie's voice calling after me. Longing tore through me, then it all spun away. I was spiraling downward, and my whole concept of myself was disintegrating, ripped apart by accelerating gravity.

Why was I here? *Was* I actually here? And what did it all mean?

I'd had bad hangovers in the past, but this was the first accompanied by existential nausea.

"Morning, Becky." Nestor, the lot guy, spritzed cleaning fluid on a windshield.

"Morning, Nestor." I tried to return his broad, white smile.

He wiped the glass with a rag, and wiped it again to remove the streaks. "Beautiful day."

"Beautiful."

Nestor threw the rag over his shoulder. From a holster he wore around his waist, he pulled out a long, looped-yarn mop with which he dusted the car. Armed with three different squirt bottles of cleaning fluid, several rags and his mop, he worked from car to car. By evening, the cars would be dull with road grime, fingerprints and streaks. Tomorrow morning, Nestor would come along and give them back their gleam. Same thing, day in and day out. Nestor seemed not to notice the repetitive futility of his work.

Actually, I guess it wasn't futile at all. As Squatty says, "If it don't shine, it don't sell."

As I watched Nestor, I could feel how much pleasure he took in his work, how the completion of each car was an accomplishment for him. I envied the concreteness and honesty of his job. Not to romanticize menial labor or anything, but his attitude made all the difference.

Certainly, there were events of larger significance than the sale or purchase of an automobile. There were things in this world of greater consequence than lesbian relationships. But what those things *were,* exactly, I wasn't sure.

Selling a car and being attracted to a woman were small things. But if even the smallest thing was purposeless, then everything was purposeless. I had no proof of this, naturally. Nor did anyone have proof of the contrary. It was a matter of choosing to believe that my life had some sort of purpose. The same must be true for everyone, I thought. Every person, every love, every car—new or used—had far-reaching implications. The way I stood on the display platform and clutched my battery-acid vending-machine coffee, for instance, made a crucial difference in the fabric of our shared reality. *If it doesn't, well, then, I'm an idiot. We're all idiots. And what's the use?*

But that's no way to live.

I sipped my coffee and watched the boulevard traffic roar past. I felt like someone stranded on a desert island, staring out at the glinting waves, praying for a rescue ship. I needed to be saved from myself.

A car pulled up to the curb. Was it Linnie's car? "Incoming!" I shouted. I felt embarrassed. Maybe I *am* hallucinating.

Her hair was impossibly golden. Her figure so willowy. Her eyes so deep blue that suddenly my desert island became a glamorous beach on the azure coast of southern France.

She is real, I thought. *Real as my punching heart.*

I hopped off the platform and met her mid-lot.

She stood less than two feet away and looked straight into my eyes. Her gaze didn't flinch, didn't wander to my mouth the way it sometimes did.

It was hard for me to meet her intense focus. I wanted to study her face, the light freckles on her nose. But I looked into her steady eyes, wordless, and could hardly bear it.

What does this woman want from me?

Then her gaze fell like a soft kiss on my mouth.

I held out my hand. "Welcome to Southland Auto Acres. I'm Becky Pine."

Linnie squinted with displeasure. She didn't shake my hand. "Don't play games."

"You're telling *me* not to play games? What can I show you today? Cars? Vans? Trucks?"

"I came to see if you're OK. I think you could press charges against Joy. I mean, not that you should. Are you feeling OK?"

"Lin, I'm not the kind of person who goes around pressing charges."

The thought of charges, let alone pressing them, hadn't even occurred to me. I felt that I deserved or needed to be thrashed by Joy as some sort of penance for having slept with Marta. Getting my ass kicked helped me atone for all the poor choices I had made.

"I mean, not that I *shouldn't* press charges," I said. "But I won't."

"You did them a favor," Linnie said. "Joy finally threw Marta out of the house. That's what Marta wanted all along, I think. Neither of them had had the courage to end it. They'll be much happier now."

I laughed, skeptical. "I thought they were staying together for Cyril's sake."

"You didn't know them before things went sour," Lin said. "They were both so smart and funny. You would have liked them when they were in love."

Linnie and I looked at each other for a moment.

"I feel horrible, Beck, about what happened to you," she said.

"Is that really why you're here, Lin? Because you feel bad?"

"Becky, I was meaning to tell you. Samuel and I are

engaged. That's what I wanted to say last night."

Her diamond ring sparkled in the sunlight. It was platinum with an enormous rock. Why hadn't I noticed it before?

"Nice ring," I said, bitter. I might as well have said, *Does Samuel know that you slept with Marta? Does he know that you're attracted to me? Can you even acknowledge these facts yourself?*

Linnie thought I was mocking her, and I guess I was. Her icy glare let me know that I had crossed the invisible line, beyond which our friendship would diminish rapidly.

"OK, then. I'm here to shop for an engagement gift," she said. "For my fiancé."

"Fine." I started walking.

She strolled alongside. "He has a few cars, but they're so *valuable*," she sighed. "I want to get him something he can slum in. Something he can park at the airport."

"Then you've come to the right place, uh… what did you say your name is?"

I heard her teeth clench. "Why don't you get used to calling me Mrs. Samuel Feldman."

"Lin, you're an asshole."

She closed her eyes as if conceding the point.

Why do I have to react like a wounded adolescent? I should just be cool. She was with me now, for whatever reason. She had come here to see me and was walking beside me now. Wasn't that enough?

I led her to the gold BMW. "This is Sweet Dream. She's my refuge. Can't even guess how many hours I've leaned on her." I was about to go into my features-and-benefits patter to build the perceived value of the vehicle before showing Lin the scarred side of the car, for which I had prepared a convincing speech about how the damage looks worse than it really is. But I just couldn't do the routine.

Freshly groomed by Nestor, the car shone as bright as Linnie's diamond.

"I fell in love with this car at first glance," I told Linnie. "From this angle, she's perfect, huh?"

Lin nodded, looking at me as much as at the car.

"But look at this." I led her to the other side. "From here, she's a wreck. I think I love this side the best. Sometimes I look at her all beat up like this and I wonder what the hell happened. I spend hours going through speculative scenarios. I used to think that if she were mine I'd fix her up, good as new. But now I don't think so. I like that I can see her wounds. It hasn't always been a Sunday drive for her. She has a past I can't ever really know and a purpose greater than I can fathom."

So far so good.

"I could own this car, hold the title to her, sure. But that's just a piece of paper. She has a soul that no one can own. I wouldn't cover that up with a thick, stupid coat of paint. Not for a million dollars or a diamond ring or the hollow approval of total strangers who call themselves society. If you love somebody you accept—"

I bit off my words. I could feel my face flush, hot and

red. I couldn't look at Linnie, even though I knew she wanted me to.

Lin stepped closer to the car. "Can we take her for a drive?"

I shrugged. "Sure." I went into the showroom to get the keys and the temporary license plate.

"Demo?" Squatty asked.

"Yeah," I said. "I really want this deal."

"Did you qualify her?"

"Squatty, this is my deal. Give me room."

He wagged his head.

I initialed the sign-out sheet and slid it across his desk. He slid the keys to me and nodded. I took this to mean that he was giving me room and, maybe, was secretly pleased that I had asked for it.

Outside, I saw that Linnie was already sitting in the passenger seat. I slipped the dealership license plate on the dashboard and got in the car. "She's automatic, as you can see," I said as I pulled toward the exit. "Fully equipped with an on-board computer that calculates your miles per gallon, average driving speed and much, much more." I was supposed to turn on the radio to demo the sound system, but I felt it would be an intrusion. I drove toward the freeway. "I needed to drive it off the lot," I explained. "But we can switch places now if you want."

"No," she said. "This way I can look at you."

"Is that a flirtation?" We stopped at a red light. "If you're flirting with me, I think that's in very, very bad taste, considering everything."

She touched my arm for a moment then withdrew her hand. She opened the glove compartment, saw that it was empty and closed it again.

The light changed, and I drove toward the freeway. "Do you have something for your hair?" I asked. "So it doesn't blow everywhere. Or should I put the top up?"

She took a few pins out of her purse and smoothed her hair back into a chignon.

The light was red, so I had a chance to look at her. "How do you do stuff like that?" I marveled. "You just snap your fingers and all of a sudden you're Grace Kelly in *To Catch a Thief*."

"It's easy." She fished around in her bag. She leaned over. Half kneeling on the car seat, she stroked my hair.

"What are you doing?"

"Hold still," she said. "This is not a flirtation. I'm fixing your hair."

The guy in the car behind me leaned on his horn. The light was already turning yellow when I sped through it.

Trying to merge on to the screaming Santa Monica freeway while Linnie styled my hair was as close as I've ever come to experiencing the fear of death and the ecstasy of erotic passion simultaneously.

I managed to get into a lane. Linnie finally sat down.

"Seat belt, please," I said.

She grudgingly complied. She was staring at me, grinning. "You look very girlie."

It was strange to feel her admiring me. I was more accustomed to staring at her, admiring her beauty. I kept my eyes on the road.

"I like it," she said. I felt her eyes disengage from me as she, too, looked through the windshield. "Samuel likes it when I wear my hair like this."

"Samuel, Samuel, Samuel. Why can't he be Sam like a regular guy?"

"He's dignified. He's Samuel."

"Linnie, sometimes I think you want to marry a man and be rich and be dignified more than you want to be happy."

"You don't understand. You can't. He respects me. Our relationship is based on respect."

"What is your relationship with Marta based on?"

"I'm sorry for you, Becky. You look at things and you think there's some big meaning behind everything. What happened with Marta meant nothing. If anything, I did it for Samuel's sake. I wanted to be certain that I'm not attracted to women. Now I'm sure. I was thinking about Samuel the whole time."

"Lin, maybe, on some level, you believe that load of crap. But I'm not fooled. Why did you come see me today?"

"I wanted to make sure there were no misunderstandings."

"Oh, please, Lin. You are crazy about me. You have no idea what to do with yourself. You want me, don't you? That's what you came to say, isn't it?"

She was quiet for what seemed like a long time. "I came

to explain." She sounded both defensive and sad.

"What is there to explain? I think it's pretty simple. Samuel has asked you to marry him, and you're freaking out. You're scrambling for an exit strategy. You're not sure you want to spend the rest of your life with him, or with anyone for that matter. You're attracted to women and you worry that maybe, just maybe, you're a lesbian. But no, heavens no, that would be a fate worse than death — or at least a level of complication that you're not willing to tackle. So you're clinging to Samuel for safety, security and legitimacy. But it doesn't feel quite right, does it?"

"Don't badger me, Becky. You think you can come barging into my psyche and throw things around anytime you feel like it. I'm asking you to please stop. Stop probing. Stop analyzing. You're like a bull in a china shop." Her head tilted back, her eyes closed. She seemed weary.

I thought of Squatty glancing at the clock and wondering what had happened to me. "I really should get back to work." I took my foot off the gas and drifted toward an exit. "I could've kidnapped you if I wanted," I said, joking, trying to lighten things up. "We could've been sipping drinks poolside in Vegas in no time."

"Becky," she said. "Now that we're engaged, Samuel and I are moving to Manhattan. Next week. It's all arranged. You probably won't see me again."

My foot hesitated for a moment. Then I hammered the gas to the floor. Sweet Dream sprinted into the center lane. I had no idea where we were going. All that mattered was that Linnie and I were going forward, going fast, together.

I drove past the skyscrapers of downtown LA. After a few miles of industrial-looking scenery, the landscape changed into an endless succession of retail-warehouse superstores, chain restaurants, and mini-malls. After that, there were some hills, then nothing but California desert. Linnie and I were backtracking along the route I had taken from Denver to LA.

Linnie's eyes were closed. There was something hopeless and defeated about the slope of her mouth. She hadn't said a word or even shifted her posture. She was moving to New York in a week. She looked as if she were surrendering herself to a grim fate. Maybe she was glad that I had stolen her and was whisking her into the desert.

What if, more than anything, she wants to run away with me? What if she doesn't want to open her eyes for fear that this is all a dream?

I wondered, too, if I wasn't dreaming. Earlier that morning I felt as if I were caught in a graveyard spiral, plummeting toward doom. But now I was simply falling like a rock through clear, calm water. The water itself was an embrace. My motion through it was effortless and thrilling. I could feel Linnie near me, beside me, surrounding me. She was nowhere and everywhere all at once.

And then I heard a voice that shook me like a depth charge: "Where's that weaksuck greenpea?"

Squatty. He was worried sick, I'll bet, calling the police, signing my termination papers. I steered toward an exit. And I was struck with a brain-freezing realization.

"Linnie?"

"What?" She didn't open her eyes.

"Can I borrow your phone?"

"What for?" She looked at me, blinking.

"I have to call my boss. My bag and all my stuff, all my money, is back at the showroom.

Her eyes narrowed with amusement. "You mean you're expecting me to finance my own abduction?"

"Would you mind?"

She reached for her purse and pulled out a cell phone. "This one's on Sam."

"I wish you'd stop bringing him up, Lin."

"Becky, he might as well be sitting in the back seat. Can we stop for a Coke?"

I pulled into the nearest gas station.

"Where are we going anyway?" Lin asked.

I put the car in park and killed the engine. "I'm taking you home to Denver to meet my parents."

"Becky, you're *not* serious."

I couldn't tell if she was intrigued or appalled. "I don't know, Lin. Wherever. We're going to the desert. To Vegas."

She handed me the phone. We both got out of the car.

"We can go back," I said. "We don't have to go anywhere."

She didn't hesitate. "Becky, I want to go." She turned and walked into the convenience store.

"All right, then," I said. "We're going."

I dialed the number. "Hi. It's Becky Pine. Let me talk to Squatty."

A minute of muzak.

A slow, untroubled voice. "This is Squatty Verlaine. What can I do ya for?"

"Squatty? It's Becky. Everything's fine."

Silence.

"Squatty?"

"I'm giving you room." I could hear him suppress a chuckle. "Go ahead and take your little lesbian joyride in a Southland Auto Acres vehicle. I can't tell you what that's done for the morale of all the fellas here. Better than a double bonus Sunday."

"Jeez, Squatty." I pressed my palm into my forehead, mortified. "That's so *creepy*."

"Gil says your girlfriend is a topless dancer."

"She's not my girlfriend." I was about to add, *And she's not a topless dancer*. But what the hell. "I'll give you a full report when I get back."

He sighed. "Take your time."

"Thank you, Squatty." I shuddered as I hung up the phone. I wished he had chewed me out. Instead, he had cast a tawdry pall over the whole trip. No matter how profound my feelings for Linnie were, most car salesmen would see the relationship as nothing more than a pulpy porn fantasy.

A few minutes later, Linnie appeared with a shopping bag.

"What'd you buy?"

"Necessities."

"Like what?"

"For later." She put the bag on the back seat. "I should call Samuel."

Every time she said his name it was like a kick in the gut. But she was right. She should call him. I handed her the phone.

I slouched into the driver seat. I tried to look like I wasn't listening to her conversation.

She turned her back to me. I couldn't hear what she was saying. What struck me, what scalded me, actually, was the babyish singsong in her voice. I had never heard that before. I burned, jealous. *She never talks to me as if I'm an adorable puppy.* After a few minutes, her tone grated on me. *Enough already.* Under the disarming melody of her voice was a manipulative bass riff.

Linnie turned and glanced at me. "With a friend," she said. "Her name is Becky." After a moment, she added, "No one, Samuel." Then she was quiet for a long time. "Yes, Samuel." He was giving her orders. She replied dutifully. "No, Samuel. Twenty-four hours. Of course, Samuel."

Then she smiled at me. "I love you, too." That was the first thing she had said in her normal Linnie voice, as if she were saying it to me.

She got in the car, buckled her seat belt. "We have one full day of adventure. So let's go," she said.

A full day would be more than enough time to convince her to leave Samuel and get together with me, I was sure. "Fine." I revved the engine. "You don't sound like yourself when you talk to him, you know." I pulled onto the road. "It's like you're bargaining with a child. If you ever talk to me like that, I'll be really insulted."

"Becky, people in adult relationships understand that there are certain compromises that have to be made and certain ways of communicating. *You*, on the other hand. You just vomit your feelings all over the place. Where does that get you?"

I merged onto the highway and jumped into the fast lane. "It gets me 24 hours with you."

"*I* got you 24 hours with me."

"Oh, this is really sick. Samuel owns you and you have to negotiate to get a day for yourself?"

"You don't understand. When you make a commitment to someone, you have a responsibility to put the priorities of the relationship above your own."

"I hope you're not the only one in the relationship who's making compromises."

"Becky, I've worked hard to have a successful relationship. It's easy for you to criticize. You don't know how much I've struggled. You weren't there to see all the tears I've cried."

We drove.

"Did you ever see that silent movie about the two guys in the desert?" Lin asked, finally. "Where one guy has a stolen bag of gold and his long-time nemesis tracks him through Death Valley?"

It sounded familiar. "Is that the one where there's a love triangle?"

"Yeah," she said. "*Greed*."

"Right, yeah. Erich Von Stroheim." I tried to remember the story line. Two guys fall in love with the same woman. One guy graciously bows out so the two can get married. Then the woman wins a lot of money in a lottery. Instead of spending any of it, she becomes a miser. Her personality becomes distorted by the gold. The marriage deteriorates. Meanwhile, the guy who bowed out of the triangle feels that he has been cheated out of a fortune.

"I like the part where the wife is living in squalor," Lin said. "She pulls out a bag of gold coins and pours them into her bed. She sleeps with her money like a lover."

"You *liked* that part?" I asked. "You mean you can *relate* to it?"

She sighed. "No, I mean, I think it's interesting. To her, the money isn't a *means*, it's an end in itself."

"It's *the* end," I said. "Because that's when her husband murders her, steals the money and escapes into the desert." I glanced over at her. "Then the other guy, the jilted guy, hunts him down."

"That last scene was haunting," Linnie said.

I gripped the wheel harder, feeling the air around us getting hot. *Two people driven by avarice and thwarted love in the desert with no water and no chance of survival.* I suddenly wanted to stop again and get something to drink.

"The irony is that one kills the other," I said. "But they're handcuffed together. Their fates are intertwined. They're inescapably interconnected in the heart of an unrelieved void."

"No, the irony is that the gold is useless to them both," Linnie corrected. She reached over and grasped my wrist, a gesture that struck me as odd. "Can you imagine dying in the desert, handcuffed to your sworn enemy, all for nothing?"

I thought for a moment. "No, Lin. I can't."

Why all his talk about greed, love and death? I confess that I was suddenly a little afraid. Linnie's true intentions were a mystery to me. Besides, I knew almost nothing about her, really.

Maybe I was being taken for a ride.

For several minutes I pondered — Why would Linnie want me dead? At first the question seemed ridiculous. But little things added up, such as her sudden hostility toward "dykes" that night at The Well. And the way she had turned on me, accusing, outside the bar. When I told her I had seen her with Marta, she was angry. Maybe she feared that Samuel would find out about her tryst. How far would she go to ensure my silence?

I studied her out of the corner of my eye. She didn't look like a killer. She came to the car lot because she was worried about me. That's what she had said. She wanted to make sure I was OK. But what if there was a dark motive hidden under the appearance of a good one? She wouldn't necessarily be aware of her murderous desire. No one is ever really conscious of his or her dark motives, are they?

I was not beyond dark motives myself. When Linnie said that I might not see her again, I wanted to say: *No, you can't; you have to stay with me.* I wanted to steal her freedom. Oh, sure, I wanted her to be happy and free, of course, just as I wanted to be happy and free myself. But in that moment I wanted to own and control her. That was the first time I had glimpsed the ugly potential of my feelings for her.

"Linnie, I have to ask you something," I said. "I need you to answer candidly."

"Sure." She turned. "What?"

"What do you want from me?"

She looked at me for a long time. "Becky, I really don't know." She reached over and put her hand on the back of my neck. "Whatever it is, it feels important. I want to figure it out. That's why we're going to Vegas."

"This whole thing, Lin, about you and Marta. About my seeing you guys together."

"That makes me a little afraid of you, Becky. Spying on us. That's stalker behavior. That's weird."

"It was stupid of me, I admit. But I wasn't stalking anyone. I was trying to see if Marta was home."

"Are you in love with her?"

"Not at all," I said. "If anything, I'm in love with you."

She moved her hand away from my neck. "Please don't say that."

"So are *you* in love with Marta?"

"Maybe I was looking for an exit strategy. Maybe you're right about that. Marriage is huge, Becky." She shook her head. After a minute, she laughed, rueful. "If there's a confused woman who needs to get laid, you can count on Marta to pounce on the opportunity, bless her heart. I don't love her. I don't even know if I love Samuel."

My heart skipped, suddenly hopeful.

"Becky, if I were to tell him I'm having second thoughts, he'd scoff. I've done too good a job convincing him that we have a happy relationship. He just wouldn't believe me."

"Tell him about you and Marta. Wouldn't that make him furious?"

"I'm afraid it would only make him horny." Linnie considered. "If I tell him, I'll have to pick the right time."

"That pisses me off," I said, still smarting from what Squatty had said on the phone. "Why do men insist that relationships between women are somehow not real? They think it's just about sex—and somehow the sex is for *their* sake."

"Becky, it's posturing. Men are terrified that women don't need them. They minimize lesbian relationships because they need to minimize the perceived threat. Besides, lesbian relationships *aren't* real."

I was stunned. "Is that some half-baked bullshit theory of yours? Like *enlightened carnality*?"

She socked me in the arm hard enough to let me know that I had hurt her feelings. "Enlightened carnality may be half baked, but it's not bullshit."

I took my foot off the gas and pulled to the side of the road. "Not real?" I said. I put the car in park and turned to her. "This thing that's not real — this imaginary love for women — has turned my life inside out." I feared that I might sock her back, so I unbuckled my seatbelt and got out of the car. "This feeling," I said as I walked around to the passenger side. "This feeling is real. This feeling is the only thing I know that is real. I love women, Linnie. This is not a game to me." I looked out at the bleak horizon and wanted to run toward it.

"I know," Lin said. She got out of the car. "Becky, please."

"Please *what*? What do you want? This is all a game to you, isn't it?"

"It's not, Becky." She reached toward me, but then stopped herself. "Please let's get back in the car."

I wanted to run until my bones were beat to dust.

"I'll drive," Linnie said. After a few moments, she opened the passenger door. "Please. Let's make this trip together."

I looked at her, into her intense eyes. She needed something from me, something that only I could provide.

"Becky, please."

I got back into Sweet Dream.

Linnie took the driver seat. "It's real," she said, "but in a different way." She gathered her thoughts. "Women are…." she began. "You. I'm talking about you, Becky. You are different."

"Different than what?"

Linnie sighed and half smiled. "Let's say there's a beautiful rose, a wild rose, growing in the middle of nowhere. Its fragrance is powerful and attracts people. People are drawn to this rose, but they don't know why. They even admire the sharpness of the thorns. It has nothing to do with reason or rationality. This rose is just unconsciously beautiful and perfect in its own way. Those who see it love it."

"Am I this rose?" I asked. "Is that what you're saying? Because that's not my experience."

"Becky, you *are* that rose. But there's another rose, too. This rose has been engineered to meet the highest rose standards. By every measure, it's perfect. It wins prizes and acclaim because it conforms to all the rules and regulations. Maybe its fragrance isn't as mysterious and intoxicating as the first rose. But with this rose comes the benefit of unreserved approval and acceptance."

"That's the Samuel rose, right?" I asked. "He's technically perfect. How special. But we're both beautiful in our own way," I said, sour.

She closed her eyes in frustration. "What I'm trying to say is that in terms of society, the second rose is the *real* rose. The first rose is something problematic that needs to be tamed or refined."

"Which rose do you prefer, Lin?"

She buckled her seatbelt and put the car in drive. "Right now, it's an impossible choice," she said. "It sucks that anyone would have to choose." She jumped back on the road, spitting gravel into the desert brush. "This car has great pickup. Woo."

Heat shimmered off the road.

"In car sales, the salesman makes the choice," I said. "There are usually at least three cars on the lot that will satisfy the buyer's basic criteria. To avoid all the indecisive agony, the salesman has to decide on a car, then convince the buyer that it's the right car to buy."

"That sounds incredibly manipulative," Linnie said. "No wonder people hate salesmen."

"It's not so nefarious," I said. "It requires the salesman to figure out which features and benefits will resonate with the buyer. Do they want safety and reliability? Or are they interested in something flashy? A car is a car is a car. It's a mode of transportation. Anything beyond the fundamental car-ness is just for style points."

She raised her brow. "Are you trying to suggest an analogy? People are people are people. Companionship is companionship. Gender is just for style points?"

I hadn't thought of that. "No," I said. "I doubt I'd be attracted to you if you were a man, Lin. Gender is more than style."

"I agree." She glanced over at me. "So what do you do if a buyer sees a car and falls in love with it? Do you try to dissuade him and sell him something else?"

Good question. "If the buyer has a strong inclination toward a particular car, I provide reinforcement. I offer reasons why it's the right car. Buyers are usually afraid of their initial attraction. They don't trust it. They don't trust their intuition to make wise practical decisions. They want a rationale," I explained. "Like Sweet Dream. I want her, but I have no rationale for buying her. It doesn't make any sense, but I want her just the same. If I had any respect for my intuition, I'd buy this car."

A truck roared past us. Linnie waited to answer until she didn't have to shout over the noise.

"You can't always trust your impulses," she said. "You have to moderate your feelings with reason. Without the overriding control of reason, we'd have pandemonium."

I loved her brain. I loved her confident way of expressing herself. There was something in the way she said this, though, that made me think she wanted me to refute it.

"*Would* we have chaos?" I asked. "Or would chaos be a temporary overreaction? Reason has us clamped down pretty tight. If all of a sudden we decided to put faith in intuition more than reason, maybe at first we'd be nuts, like kids who eat too much candy and get sick. But after that initial bump, who knows? What we call reason flies in the face of common sense much of the time, anyway. It's like your rose analogy. It kills me that we find it reasonable to intervene with nature and somehow make a better flower. Better *wheat*, maybe. That's common sense, provided that we are in fact making it better. But better flowers? In the meantime, we burn down the rainforest and kill flowers that we've never even seen. That's crazy, Lin. There's already pandemonium. Reason isn't helping."

"You spent too much time in Boulder," Linnie said, grinning. "I see your point. You're trying to sell me on intuition over reason. I almost bought it. Until you mentioned the rainforest," she needled, rolling her eyes.

"You almost bought it?"

She nodded. "Almost."

We drove in silence for a long time. I admired her posture. She sat straight and attentive with her hands on the wheel firmly at ten and two o'clock respectively. She looked like somebody's wife, like a mom with a car full of kids. I felt safe.

I dozed. When I opened my eyes, I saw Vegas in the distance. I thought we were only a few minutes from the strip. The hotels seemed so close. In reality, we were still several miles from town. I thought it must be a phantom city, like a carrot on a stick, dangling, enticing us, without ever allowing us to reach it.

"While you were asleep, I called ahead and got us a room at New York, New York," Linnie said.

My stomach clenched, partly because I remembered that Linnie was planning to move to New York and partly because I was hungry. "I could eat," I said.

Finally, we made it to the strip. Linnie pulled into a parking lot the size of a football stadium.

The inside of the hotel brought back memories of the last time I had checked into a hotel with a woman. At the time, I was worried about what people might think. Linnie checked us in, and I didn't care what anyone thought. Our only luggage was the small bag from the convenience store. It seemed to strike the desk clerk as strange. *We're here. We're queer. Get used to it.*

Our spacious room had one king-sized bed. "Nice," I said, sitting down on it. I'm alone with Linnie, I thought.

We are going to sleep together in this bed.

She seemed nervous.

I was terrified.

"What's in the bag?" I asked.

She produced two toothbrushes and a tube of toothpaste.

I was impressed with her foresight and dedication to dental hygiene, and wanted to say so. But I suddenly felt claustrophobic, awkward.

"We should go eat something," she said.

The casino shook with light and sound, but there was an uncomfortable silence between the two of us. We ate at an Italian restaurant. We looked at each other, but there was nothing to say. At first, I panicked and racked my brain for something to say — a stupid joke — anything. Nothing felt appropriate. Halfway through my salad, I surrendered to the awkwardness of just being there with her.

I observed with quiet astonishment that she was able to eat without smudging her lipstick and without having to wipe her mouth. She made it look effortless. I added this to the mounting pile of evidence proclaiming her absolute perfection.

It occurred to me that I was overestimating her. No one is absolutely perfect. I was exaggerating. I was idealizing her.

Maybe it's not possible to see people for who they truly are. Maybe I'm always going to misjudge them, either too favorably or too critically. How perilous and sad to live in a world, in which I never really know people accurately, not even myself.

I looked at Linnie. She was staring into the middle distance, chewing. I watched the muscles in her jaw shift.

Good or bad, perfect or not, there was more joy to be found in appreciating Linnie than in trying to analyze her impartially. I was partial toward her — biased, skewed. So what? In the presence of a woman like Lin, objective accuracy was a moronic thing to strive for.

"How's your food?" she asked.

"Fine. Yours?"

"Fine."

After dinner, we strolled through the sham streets of the Big Apple. "This is what it's going to be like when you live in Manhattan," I said.

She forced a smile. "With fewer slot machines."

The obvious thing for us to do, I thought, was to go back to our room. But I wasn't ready. I stopped in front of an Elvis machine. "I want to play this," I said. "It feels lucky."

"Look at the payouts," Lin said. "They're not very generous. Besides, this isn't real gambling."

"I have a feeling about this, Lin. It's an intuition thing."

She handed me twenty bucks. "When this runs out, come find me. I'm going to play craps."

We parted, and I was relieved. I didn't know how to break the tension between us. She was probably as nervous as I was about the prospect of the two of us sleeping together.

A half hour passed. Linnie came back to where I was

sitting. "I'm having no luck," she said.

"I'm doing OK. I managed to play this whole time on twenty bucks."

Linnie pulled up a stool and sat down next to me. "You're almost out of money."

"I know, but Elvis wants to give me a big payout. I can feel it." I spun the reels a couple of times. I had enough left for just one more spin.

"On the last spin I like to say, *Nam-myoho-renge-kyo*," I said.

"What's that?"

"A lucky Buddhist mantra."

She rolled her eyes. We said it in unison. I spun the reels.

We lost.

"It doesn't work," I shrugged. "Or else its effects are extremely subtle."

"It works," Linnie said. "I wanted you to stop playing this stupid machine." She smiled. "My prayer has been answered."

I laughed. "We both want different things, huh?"

"Maybe," she said. "I need to stop worrying about my future and just enjoy my time here with you."

"Yeah, me too." I held out my hand. "Deal?"

We shook hands. "Deal," she said.

Things felt good between us again.

"How do you play craps?" I asked. "Is the object of the game to get *crap*?"

"Let me show you."

The craps table was a sea of confusion ringed by people shouting, flinging chips and throwing dice. I stood next to Lin as she placed her bets. I noticed that every so often, she would place a chip in front of me on the pass line. Other people rolled the dice. After a while, she said, "You're bringing me luck."

I wondered how that was possible — I didn't understand the game. I had no idea what made a roll of the dice good or bad. Seven was significant — whether good or bad, though, I could not discern. Mathematics were apparently involved, so my brain switched off.

"Good or bad all depends on your bet," Linnie said. She put a chip on the pass line in front of me. "It's your turn."

The croupier pushed a selection of dice toward me.

"No, Linnie. I can't. I've never done this before."

The man next to me said, "Green shooter." He placed a stack of chips on the felt. "Seven."

There was suddenly a heightened anticipation around the table. People called out more bets.

"Choose two dice," Linnie instructed. "You're lucky because you're not trying for anything. Just roll and hope for the best." She placed her bet.

I took the dice and shot.

The croupier called out a number. The guy next to me cheered. Chips clacked and moved around the table.

"Was that good?" I asked.

"Keep rolling."

I rolled for what seemed like a very, very long time. My hands were sweaty. Linnie and others were accumulating stacks of chips. People were yelling different numbers. They were looking at me, shouting encouragement that sounded like threats. "Five, shooter, give me five." The pressure was excruciating.

I rolled again. The table exploded with cheers.

I grabbed Linnie's arm. "That's it," I said. "I'm going to roll a seven. I know it. I can feel it."

"You're not going to roll a seven," she said.

"Take your chips off, Lin."

"Becky, I'm going to trust *my* intuition this time." She took a tall stack of chips and placed it on the table. She called out her bet.

The guy next to me said, "Ooooh." Someone else said, "Betting the horn."

"*This* is gambling, Becky. I'm betting on you."

"Don't, Lin. Please."

She put her lips to my ear and said, "Give me boxcars."

Her voice sent a tingle down my neck and down my arm. I felt it in my fingers as I released the dice.

The guy next to me shouted, "Ho *ho*!"

I rolled twelve. Two sixes. Apparently, that's what Linnie meant by boxcars.

She gathered her considerable winnings. "Now you can roll a seven."

I rolled.

Seven.

We were giddy, laughing and drinking martinis in a hotel bar. Linnie had cashed in most of the chips. She handed me a wad of money.

"I don't want that," I said, giving it back to her.

"But you won it."

"Linnie, you won it." I shrugged. "Give it to Samuel."

Her smile seemed to fade. "I can't remember when I've had so much fun," she said.

"We have a spark." I drained my glass. "I want to kiss you, Lin. But I'm scared. I'm scared that I won't want to stop. And I'm scared that it won't make any difference. You'll leave me anyway."

She listened, serious.

"But I'm also scared to *not* kiss you. If we don't kiss, and you leave, I'll always have an idealized view of you. You'll be my great unrequited love who haunts me because, tragically, we never even kissed."

After a moment, she said, "It's a dilemma." She ordered another round of drinks.

We both sat silently for a while but without any awkwardness.

"It's not about sex," she said. "My relationship with Samuel is not about sex." She stirred her drink with an olive on a toothpick. "My feelings for you are maybe *more* about sex. But it's not about sex." She ate the olive. "It's not about curiosity either. Marta pretty much answered all my questions."

I winced at the thought. I drank.

"I care about you, Becky. You matter to me. Beyond that, I don't know. I don't know what to do with that feeling. I don't know how to fit it into my life. But it's there." She pressed her palm to her heart. "It's here."

I believed her. I drank more. She could never marry Samuel. No way. I was certain of it. We had a lot to talk about on our drive back to LA.

"I'm getting sleepy," I said.

"Me too."

Back in our room, I wasn't nervous. I brushed my teeth. When Lin went into the bathroom, I took off my clothes and slid between the sheets. I turned off the bedside light. A few minutes later, Linnie came out of the bathroom. In the dark, she walked past the bed and opened the drapes a little, letting a hint of neon light into the room.

I watched her undress. She got into bed.

The silence between us was electric. More than anything, I wanted to kiss her. Somehow, though, it didn't seem right.

I propped myself on my elbow and looked at Lin. "It feels like we're not alone," I said. "In a way, it feels like Samuel and Marta are here, too."

"Yeah," she whispered. She looked at me for what felt like a long time. "When you make love with someone maybe it binds you to that person in a way deeper than anyone can understand."

I dropped my head back on the pillow. "Maybe," I said, considering. "The depth of it probably depends on the sincerity of your feeling."

"Becky." She pressed herself on top of me.

The sudden, perfect contact of our bodies — the smooth completeness — startled us both. Her gaze deepened, almost tearful.

Our kiss was oceanic.

I wanted to push her away and pin her down at the same time. I rolled on top of her, both of us wrestling to get closer to each other.

She froze. "I can't," she said. She turned away from me. "Becky, we just can't." She curled up on her side.

I wasn't sure how to respond. I touched my lips to her shoulder and thought about it. Maybe this wasn't the best time for us. Technically, she and Samuel were still together. Plus, the image of her on Marta's bed was still fresh in my mind.

"It's OK," I said. "Being near you is almost too intense anyway." I hoped she would say something. She made a sound like a sob.

I moved away from her and stared at the ceiling. She had said: *When you make love with someone maybe it binds you to that person in a way deeper than anyone can understand.* She was right; we probably weren't ready for that yet.

"It's OK, Lin," I said. "We don't need to rush."

I slept as if I would be sleeping beside her for the rest of my life—a long, contented rest.

In the morning, I woke up. Alone.

Linnie had left me some casino chips. She had written a note: "I am flying back to LA this morning. This is for the best. I figured out what I want from you, Becky. I am going to marry Samuel. What I want is something you probably don't want to give, but it's important to me, and maybe important to you, too. I want your blessing. Love, Linnie."

My blessing? Was she kidding? What about our 24 hours together? I didn't even get a full 24. She chose Samuel over me. She abandoned me without so much as goodbye. She signed it, *Love, Linnie*. Was she being ironic?

My *blessing*?

Yeah, that's rich. Ha fucking ha ha.

I looked at Vegas in my rearview mirror. It *was* a phantom city. In broad daylight, all of its magic was gone.

There was a story, an ancient tale, about a group of travelers walking across a desert. The journey had become harder than anyone had anticipated. Everyone was exhausted but there was nowhere to rest. Just as the travelers were about to give up and collapse, their guide shouted that they were nearing a city. Sure enough, the travelers suddenly found themselves in a luxurious palace. They rested and were refreshed. In the morning, they woke up to find that the city had vanished. The phantom city appeared when they needed it, giving them strength to continue their journey.

Maybe Lin was my phantom girlfriend, helping me get where I needed to go, wherever that was. She had vanished, but I didn't feel refreshed or grateful. I felt cheated.

The drive back to LA was long. I took it slow, stewing the whole way.

By the time I got to Southland Auto Acres, the place was closed. I parked Sweet Dream in the car wash bay, unlocked the showroom, and got my stuff.

I was done with LA, women and life. I thought about leaving a resignation letter on Squatty's desk, but I was too tired to write.

On the pavement near my car, I noticed two cigar butts. I figured that Reynolds and Gil had waited around for me to show up. I imagined them sharing a smoke and some guy-to-guy talk. Good for that, I thought. *Good for them.* Maybe they worked out their mutual jealousy issues and were now having passionate sex. I smiled and grimaced at the thought. *Anything is possible.*

The next day, I decided that I should go back to work. My decision was influenced primarily by the fact that there was nothing I wanted to watch on TV. I had slept in, cleaned my apartment, read the paper and found myself staring at the ceiling. By mid-afternoon, I was ready to have a life again.

Squatty was startled to see me. I must've looked like hell. "Becky, get in my office."

I sat in the chair opposite Squatty's desk, as I had done the day I met him.

He settled in across from me and prepared to light his cigar. I expected him to reprimand me for blowing off work.

"The human being is essentially a shit factory," he began. "No matter how pure at heart we may be, the basic biological fact remains that our life-sustaining processes produce shit." He eyed me. "Becky, what I'm saying is that shit is unavoidable. You can't run away from it. It follows wherever you go." He struck a match and puffed his cigar. "Some people might tell you that a car lot is a particularly shitty place, a dedicated shit depository if you will. It is. But." He stabbed his cigar toward me. "Shit is fertilizer. Shit is what makes it possible for things to grow. This is a place where a person can grow and bloom. When you understand that, then you've transformed the shit into a thing of beauty."

I sighed. "Squatty, that's a great theory. It sounds wonderful, really. But I haven't seen anything bloom for me here. All I see is disappointment. I have these dreams — mostly about finding someone who loves me and wants to be with me. I feel like it's never going to happen, Squatty. Life is just more shit on top of shit with nothing ever sprouting."

He leaned back in his chair and chuckled, amused at my melodramatic melancholy. "Becky, you can stand in a garden and shout at the flowers. You can order them to grow, tell them to bloom. But that doesn't help. You can tear out your hair and worry and drink yourself blind because your garden is not growing on schedule and to your specifications. But that won't make things grow any faster or any better. Living things have their own way. They do things in their own time and on their own terms. You have to let them."

He looked at me to see if I was encouraged by this, but I wasn't. It reminded me of Linnie's rose analogy, and it sounded like a cruel joke. I nodded, lifting one corner of my mouth. "Yeah, Squatty, whatever."

"Lookie here," he said leaning toward me. "I want you to stay at Southland Auto Acres. You're becoming a good salesman. I don't want to lose you."

"I'm not going anywhere," I said, dispirited. "I haven't thought of anything better to do with my life."

"Then get back on the line. The day's a-wasting." I was halfway out the door when he said, "And congrats on your deal this morning."

"What deal?"

"Your friend from yesterday, the pretty gal." Squatty smiled bigger than I've ever seen him smile. "She came in and bought Sweet Dream."

My face burned. *Linnie bought Sweet Dream as an engagement gift for Samuel. That bitch.*

"She told me to send the car to the body shop and fix her up better than new," Squatty said, looking puzzled as he studied my reaction. "I worked the numbers myself, but I'll give you the full deal, so don't worry about that." He seemed taken aback by the rage that was probably flaring in my eyes. "She got a good price, Becky. She told me to give you these."

He held up the keys to the car.

"Becky, she bought it for you."

I took the keys, muttered thanks. I walked outside not knowing what to think or how to feel. What did it mean? Was this a consolation prize? *I don't want a damn consolation prize. I don't want to be the also-ran.*

Plus, I liked Sweet Dream's scars and scrapes. Linnie knew that. Was she trying to smooth everything over, hide it all under a coat of paint?

I gazed out at the endless stream of traffic. I pictured myself cruising down Santa Monica Boulevard in my pristine Sweet Dream, my one true vehicle. I would never be able to drive that car without thinking of Lin. She knew that, too.

I wanted to tell myself that this lovely parting gift was a way for her to mess with my head, a mixed signal to keep me forever in her thrall—an unrequited love scenario. But I weighed those keys in my hand. They felt like a confirmation of something real and significant between Linnie and me.

The car was gravy. The important thing was the happiness I felt growing in my heart. I knew that Lin and I were connected. Nothing could change that— not geographical distance, or her marriage to Samuel, or my shouting at the garden.

I sat on the outdoor platform and wrapped those keys in my fist. I pressed them to my forehead in a gesture of prayer, *Live your life, Lin. Please be happy. I promise to do the same.* That's the best blessing I had to offer.

After a few minutes, I raised my head and looked toward the curb. Incoming.

She's mine.